HOT SEAL, UNDER PRESSURE

INCLUDES HOT SEAL, COLD WATER

CAT JOHNSON

COPYRIGHT 2022 Cat Johnson

HOT SEAL, UNDER PRESSURE

1

The tall, impeccably dressed, sophisticated woman standing at the head of the conference table was the perfect representation of what Shelly Laurens wanted to be. And everything she currently wasn't.

Joanne Rossi silently emitted power and control, wrapped in a cool sleek package. Fashionable but not trendy. Feminine while also being strong and slightly intimidating.

The executive producer of New Millennia Media was a no nonsense, get shit done kind of woman, rising to the top in a male dominated field, and Shelly wanted to be her.

For now, she'd have to settle for working for her.

"Shelly. You're up. What have you got?" Joanne asked, focusing all of her attention on Shelly just as she had been daydreaming about the day she would stand at the head of this table as the boss.

Luckily before the meeting started Shelly had rehearsed her answer for the question she knew was coming.

"So tomorrow we're filming the final episode of this season on *Trash to Treasure* with the big *Hot House* cross-over event. It'll be the reveal of Zach and Gabby's backyard makeover, while they're hosting the co-ed bridal shower for Clay and Tasha."

"I love it. Will Nick and Dani be there?" Joanne asked.

"Yes, ma'am." Shelly nodded.

She knew the three reality shows the San Diego branch of the Burbank-based production company handled were Joanne's favorite. The shows had been the reason Joanne made such frequent trips down the coast over the past couple of years.

Of course, Joanne's new SEAL boyfriend was the more recent reason for her frequent visits to Coronado.

"Perfect." Joanne looked happy, which was a very good thing. When the EP was unhappy, *everyone* was unhappy.

Shelly smiled too. The cross-over finale was going to be the event of the season and it had been all her idea.

Although she hadn't gotten a whole lot of credit or praise for it. Being an associate producer meant the producer got the public credit for her ideas.

She couldn't help but hope that would change one day soon. A raise. A promotion. A promotion that came with a raise…she'd be happy with anything.

Until then, she had to keep killing it at this job and keep herself front and center and in the good graces of the powers that be at New Millennia Media.

One of those powers was Joanne—executive producer, show runner and Navy SEAL obsessed, even before she'd met her new man. That was evidenced by the number of reality shows she'd crafted around select SEALs from Coronado during the past three seasons.

It was that SEAL obsession Shelly intended to use to get ahead in her career.

The moment she'd heard the gossip about Joanne's new beau Jacob strutting onto the set of the bridal show in his US Navy dress uniform to whisk Joanne away, Shelly's mind had begun to spin.

The romantic scene was the stuff Hollywood legends were made of—and it had all been caught on camera. Not that Joanne would ever allow her personal life to be aired. But she couldn't stop the talk, and it had given Shelly an idea. An idea she hoped would propel her from associate to full-fledged producer sooner rather than later.

Coming up with ideas for episodes was one thing. But coming up with a concept for an all new, hopefully blockbuster show—that would be tremendous.

"All right. Thanks, everybody. That's a wrap." Joanne dismissed the group and turned her attention to her cell phone.

As the meeting broke, all the other attendees scurried off to their assignments. But Shelly hung back.

"Um, Joanne." Shelly raised her hand like she was a

schoolgirl. She quickly lowered it again when she realized what she'd done.

Cell still in hand, Joanne's brows rose along with her gaze as she pinned Shelly with a stare. "Yes?"

"I have a concept for a new show." She saw Joanne's walls go up at the words.

Okay, so maybe as EP Joanne did get bombarded with show ideas all the time from everywhere and everybody. But Shelly would never get anywhere if she didn't at least try to make the pitch.

With that thought steeling her nerve, she continued.

"The concept is centered around the Navy SEAL training at Coronado," she explained, knowing SEALs were Joanne's catnip.

She saw a crack in the wall as Joanne looked a little more interested and nodded. "Go on."

"We put eight teams in competition against each other in challenges based on the SEALs' BUD/S training. Each team will be comprised of one SEAL and one civilian."

When Joanne laid her phone on the table Shelly knew she'd really gotten her attention.

"The marketing team for actor Jamey Garret's movie where he played a SEAL did something along these lines to promote the movie and bring attention to the fact they'd used actual SEALs as extras in the action scenes. They had a real Navy SEAL run the obstacle course at Coronado, and then had Jamey run the course after him. The video of it has over five million hits on YouTube. We can do that too. One SEAL and one every day, average Joe."

Joanne nodded slowly as she got a faraway look in her eyes. "Okay, but let's make all the teams be one SEAL and one *female* civilian."

Shelly's heart began to pound as it looked like her show idea might become a reality, even though she saw exactly where Joanne's mind was going.

Making the teams co-ed would add another element to the show, because of course Joanne would be hoping for romance. Or more accurately, for the team members to hook-up.

Sex sells. The old adage was true, and sex on reality shows translated to an instant ratings boost.

While Shelly had been envisioning a more athletic, action type show, such as *American Ninja Warrior* or *Wipeout*, Joanne clearly had a different idea. Shelly knew they'd cast only single, hot, young and beautiful people.

It would be more like the *Bachelor in Paradise* but with an obstacle course. That wasn't what Shelly had wanted, but it might be what she'd get. She'd have to accept that. Beggars can't be choosers.

"You know what. Let's kick it up another notch. We'll get our SEALs and their wives to fill three of the team spots."

Shelly's eyes flew wide. "Um, what?"

"Clay and Tasha, Zach and Gabby, and Nick and Dani. They'll bring in a ready-made fanbase."

If there was one thing Shelly knew for certain, it was that not one of those SEALs Joanne had mentioned was going to want to do this new show, even with their wives as partners.

"Uh, I don't—"

Obviously not hearing Shelly, or just not listening, Joanne continued speaking, "Get our couples on board, find five more camera-ready teams, and we'll start shooting the sizzle reel. We need that done right away so we can start pitching it to networks while Clay and Tasha are away on their honeymoon."

With that, Joanne left, leaving Shelly with her final protest still unspoken on her lips and with a sick feeling in her stomach. Not to mention an impossible task in front of her.

She should have never pitched the idea.

When she failed miserably at pulling it all together as Joanne had specified, it would be a catastrophic blow to her career. She should have just kept her mouth shut.

As she envisioned her hopes and dreams going down the toilet, her cell phone vibrated on the table in front of her where she'd abandoned it in her grief.

She glanced at the display and saw her best friend's name.

"Alicia. Hi," she said on a sigh.

"You don't have to sound quite so enthusiastic to be talking to me." Alicia laughed.

"Sorry. Joanne just dumped a big mess in my lap."

"You thrive on sorting out Joanne's big messes. And as usual, you'll perform some miracle. The boss will be happy and then you'll be riding an adrenaline high until the next mess comes along. Wash. Rinse. Repeat."

Her best friend knew her well, although what Alicia didn't know was the challenge she was up against.

"I'm not sure I can work a miracle this time."

"Will a drink and a bitch session at McP's help?" Alicia asked.

"God, yes." Shelly glanced at the time on her smartwatch. It was coming up on rush hour. She calculated for the traffic that would be between her and that much needed drink. "I can be there in half an hour."

"I'll be there in fifteen. I'll have a drink waiting for you. Because that's the kind of friend I am," Alicia joked.

"Yes, you are. You're the *best* friend I've ever had." Something clicked in Shelly's brain as she said the words.

Alicia was her best friend who also happened to be dating a Navy SEAL, because you couldn't throw a rock in Coronado without hitting a SEAL. And you definitely couldn't grab a drink at McP's Pub, their favorite bar, without seeing one.

It so happened that it was three very stubborn and camera-adverse Navy SEALs that Shelly had to convince to do yet another reality show when they didn't even like doing the ones they'd already been on. But maybe—just maybe—Alicia's boyfriend Brian could convince them. SEAL-to-SEAL.

And the best way to get Brian to do something, was to get Alicia to convince him to do it.

The cloud lifted from Shelly's mood as her plan formed. She might have even smiled as she pushed back her chair and stood.

Next stop, McP's Pub in Coronado.

2

"Another day, another successful hostage release." Wyatt slammed the door of his equipment cage with a sigh, not sounding as enthusiastic as the statement warranted.

With his brows raised at the unexpected attitude, Stefan Kowalski glanced at his teammate.

"Sorry the fact no one was shooting at us on this op is boring for you," Ty snorted.

Danny glanced up from where he was untying his boot laces. "Hell, I'll happily take escorting two already released hostages home over going in guns blazing and taking them out by force."

"Easy day," Eric agreed with a nod. "And not without importance. Venezuela releasing those hostages is huge. With the shit happening with Russia, we need good relations with Venezuela right now."

Mason snorted. "Yeah. Because they have oil and oil makes the world go round."

"All right, you guys. We're not solving the world's problems here and now so who's up for a drink?" Ty looked around.

Stefan shook his head. "I'm out. I've got to call home."

"Aw. Come on, Kowalski. How long will that take?" Wyatt asked.

Stefan huffed out a short laugh. "With my family? A long time."

Ty glanced up to pin Stefan with his gaze. "Hey, tell your mom thanks for the last care package. And then hint we need more."

"Your mom's homemade pierogi? Hell, yes. *Lots* more," Mason agreed.

It was becoming obvious to Stefan that sharing the contents of his care packages from his mother back home in Brooklyn with his team had been a mistake. He was paying for it now with their obsessive comments and demands, not to mention their constant stealing of his food.

Her pierogi had become his claim to fame. Nothing he'd do as a SEAL, no feat of heroism, would ever live up to the reputation of his mother's cooking.

Stefan shook his head. Time to nip this habit in the bud. "I'm not asking her for more—"

Ty pointed a finger at him. "You got us all addicted to

those damn potato things your mom makes. You can't leave us hanging."

"Okay. So it's settled. Kowalski makes his call, secures more pierogi for us, then he meets us at the bar. Sound like a plan?" Wyatt looked around.

Stefan sighed. "Maybe."

"Maybe? You got something better to do?" Eric asked.

He hadn't. Though it sucked to have to admit that. "All right. Fine. I'll meet you at McP's."

"There we go. That's what I like to see. Peer pressure at its best." Danny laughed.

The members of his team, after a few more verbal pokes and jabs, finally left.

Alone, Stefan pulled out his cell and dialed his parents' landline. The same number they'd had while he'd grown up in the house. The number they'd no doubt keep until the day they died.

It didn't matter to them that most of the rest of the world had already gotten rid of their landlines.

As he pressed the cell to his ear, he realized peer pressure would never sway his parents like it had him today.

"You missed the weekly Sunday video call," his little sister Irina said, forgoing the usual, socially accepted practice of saying *hello* when answering a call.

"I was away."

"So where were you this time?" she asked, the excitement clear in her voice.

"Training." It was his stock answer for questions like this.

Lies were easier when you had an answer prepared. Although after all the years he'd been a SEAL, he could come up with them on the fly as well. Apparently lying got easier with practice.

"I don't believe you," she said.

He laughed, picturing his sister's face screwed up in an unhappy scowl. "I don't care if you believe me or not."

"Ooo. Wait. Were you in Ukraine?" she asked, sounding every bit the recent political science college graduate that she was.

"No," he answered truthfully. Although, given the state of things there, it had been a good guess.

"Hmm. A bordering country then. Poland? Oh my God, Stefan. If you got to go to Poland and Mom and Dad haven't even been back since they left—"

"Irina. Stop. I was not in Poland. I told you. I was training."

"Yeah, sure." The comment dripped in sarcasm. "What kind of *training*?" she quizzed him, still sounding skeptical.

He could hear the air quotes she'd no doubt used as she'd said the word.

"Fast roping out of helicopters, mostly," he answered, flashing back to his last actual training.

"Mmm-hmm. And where was this *supposed* training?"

"The desert just outside of Vegas," he answered with

another truth. That training had actually happened, just not this week. Or even this year.

"If you're not lying, then I'm really jealous. Vegas? I so want to go there. You get to go to all the cool places."

He heard the pout in her voice.

"Yup. That's true. Join the SEALs, see the world. Maybe they should make that the new recruitment slogan," Stefan replied to her ridiculous statement with his own sarcastic comment. "And if you want to go to Vegas so badly, then go."

"Mom and Dad will never let me."

"You're over twenty-one. You can do whatever you want."

"Not while I'm still living under their roof for free, as they remind me so often. Besides, they would just say it's not safe. Which is why my big strong brother should take me with him."

"Yeah, don't hold your breath." He wasn't the pick up and fly to Vegas to gamble on the Strip type.

Too much traffic. Too many crowds. He'd never be able to relax there. What kind of vacation would that be?

Nope. Give him a solo run on the beach. *That* was relaxing.

"So what's going on there?" he asked, hoping for a subject change.

"Mom's been cooking up a storm, getting stuff ready for Easter."

He stifled a groan as he could almost smell the scents

that filled the house this time of year. "Sorry I'm gonna miss it."

"You won't. She's packing up a bunch of it to send to you."

Polish delicacies he'd have to share with his team, which would only encourage them to expect more. He really needed to get his own place and stop living in the bachelor barracks. It was cheap and convenient. And it offered next to zero privacy.

He just couldn't swallow paying Coronado prices for rent. And he didn't have enough saved for a down payment to buy.

The sound of a cell phone ringing interrupted his thoughts.

"That's my cell," Irina announced. "I gotta go, bro. My boyfriend's calling. I'll tell Mom and Dad you called."

"Wait! You have a boy—"

She hung up before he even finished the question or could tell her to just put one of his parents on the line, which is why he'd called to begin with.

With a sigh he disconnected and decided to try again later. Maybe during prime time on the east coast when he knew his mother would be seated in her chair in front of the television with the phone next to her as she watched whatever show was airing.

Until then, McP's awaited.

The bar was close enough to the base, it made McP's Pub the place to go for both SEALs and retirees who lived locally. The beer was cold, the food was good and the outdoor seating was a plus, especially on a perfect California day like today.

Stefan walked past the inside tables and headed to the patio, knowing the team was seated out there. He'd heard them while he'd been parking his Jeep. They weren't the quietest bunch when they got together and alcohol was involved.

"Here he is," Danny announced.

"What's the sitrep with our care package?" Mason asked.

He rolled his eyes and hated he had good news for his greedy teammates. "You're in luck. She's cooking. A package is coming."

A cheer rose among the five men, drawing a few glances from those seated at the other tables on the patio.

Stefan shook his head and couldn't help his smile. It didn't take much to make them happy. He should just let them have the win and not begrudge them the joy of his mother's cooking. It wasn't like they got a lot of home cooking while living on base.

Ty held up a beer. "A toast to our buddy Stefan Pierogi Kowalski."

"To Pierogi." Wyatt nodded.

"To Pierogi." The rest of the team raised their glasses and echoed the toast.

Stefan's eyes widened. He'd made it through boot camp and BUD/S and over a decade in the teams without picking up a nickname. He sure as hell wasn't going to let his team give him one now—especially if that name was going to be Pierogi.

He needed to nip this shit in the bud right now. "Whoa, whoa, whoa. That is not gonna become a thing."

"What isn't?" Eric asked.

"That name."

"Why not? It's perfect, *Pierogi*." Ty grinned.

"No." His Brooklyn attitude coming out, Stefan leveled a glare on each and every man in turn. "Anyone, *anyone*, who calls me that is gonna have to deal with me."

"That's a threat, is it?" Ty's brows rose high at the implied challenge.

"I do remember a certain sparring match that you lost to Ty, Pierogi," Wyatt reminded. "Are you two up for a rematch?"

He clearly had to change tactics as the dreaded name became more solidified each time someone used it. "Okay, then, how about this? Anyone who calls me that gets nothing out of that care package. Or any future care packages."

"I think your mother would be interested in knowing you're being selfish. In fact, I think she'd probably send us our own package once we tell her you're not sharing," Eric threatened, his arms crossed over his chest.

They were probably right, and he wouldn't be surprised if these bastards did contact his mother. His home address was no secret.

"And, once we have established a rapport with your mother, it's just a matter of time before me and your hot sister start talking," Ty, whose nickname was Flirt for good reason, threatened.

That was not going to happen. Not on his watch.

Stefan narrowed his eyes at them, his chest rising and falling as he drew in an angry breath as the situation spiraled more out of his control.

Then an idea formed.

He might have lost that sparring match against Ty, but there was one place he dominated. Always had, since BUD/S. The O-Course.

"Okay. How about this?" He glanced around at the group.

"Me against all of you on the O-Course. Fastest time takes it. If I win, no one calls me Pierogi ever again."

"And if one of us wins, we can all call you that all we want *and* we get whatever is in that next care package," Eric challenged him.

"Fine." Stefan nodded. He wasn't concerned. There was no way they were winning this.

"I'm in," Mason agreed.

"Me too. When are we doing this?" Danny asked.

"Tomorrow. Zero-nine-hundred. Or do you slowpokes need a few days to train?" Stefan joked.

"No, we don't need a few days to train," Wyatt said, mimicking Stefan while screwing up his face unhappily.

"Sounds good." Stefan glanced around for a waitress.

He needed a beer to celebrate. Tomorrow morning he'd be rid of this new nickname and he'd be the undisputed king of the O-Course. He couldn't wait.

3

"No."

Shelly frowned. "What do you mean, no? I didn't even ask the question yet."

Brian shook his head. "I don't need to hear the question. I can tell already that it involves me and you and SEALs from the base so the answer is no."

Shelly pouted and looked to Alicia for help. Brian was Alicia's boyfriend after all.

Her friend shook her head. "Don't look at me. After the last disaster, I'm staying out of it."

"It wasn't a disaster." Shelly pouted.

"It wasn't?" Alicia's dark brows shot high. "I got Brian to fix you up with one of his SEAL friends and you pretended to get an emergency phone call and ditched him halfway through the date."

"Yeah. That." Brian pointed to Alicia and nodded.

Shelly scowled. "That wasn't my fault."

"Oh? Whose fault was it? There were only two of you on the date and you were the one who left so..." Alicia wobbled her head back and forth.

"There were extenuating circumstances," Shelly said in defense.

She'd already had a bit of a crush on another guy when the date she'd been pushing Alicia and Brian to set up suddenly was happening.

She'd gone and she shouldn't have, because her heart and her mind were with another guy the whole time. So she'd decided to cut her losses and ended the night early. Before she'd ordered dinner and ran up the bill any higher, which she'd thought was nice of her.

As it turned out, she shouldn't have written off Brian's friend so quickly because the guy she'd thought she had a thing for turned out to be a two-timing bastard.

Hence the reason she was currently single and *not* looking.

But her sorry single status didn't have anything to do with her SEAL problems now. She needed five SEALs for the reality show and she had to somehow convince Clay, Zach and Nick to do it too.

It all seemed hopeless. She sighed.

Brian cocked up a brow. "Looking pitiful won't make me help you."

"I'm not trying to look pitiful on purpose. I just am."

He sighed. "Okay. Tell me what you need."

She perked up, eyes widening as she leaned forward.

"Softie," Alicia mumbled to her boyfriend.

Brian shot Alicia a sideways glance. "I didn't say I'd help. But maybe I can offer some advice."

"I'll take advice." She'd take anything she could get at this point.

Shelly explained the show concept and Joanne's decree, as well as the challenges it presented.

When she was done, she asked, "Any ideas?"

Brian scowled. "I hate that I do, but yes, I have a couple of ideas."

"Oh my God. Thank you."

"Hang on. No guarantees," he warned.

She shook her head. "No guarantee needed."

"All right. For the SEALs who have already been in your reality shows—I've seen a couple of episodes and I've seen them hanging around here. Even though I don't know them well, I know their type. You should appeal to Clay first. He's the oldest."

"He's also the most stubborn," Shelly pointed out. Not to mention borderline scary sometimes.

Brian nodded. "That may be, but he's the most competitive. You challenge him. Appeal to his competitive nature. Let him know that if he doesn't do this, it's going to look like he's afraid of losing. He'll rise to the challenge. And when he does, the others will follow."

"You really think so?" Shelly asked.

"I do." Brian nodded.

Alicia glanced at her boyfriend. "That's pretty brilliant."

"Why, thank you." Brian beamed.

Shelly was pretty ecstatic herself that her psychiatrist best friend thought this was a good idea. One that would work.

One problem down. One to go.

"What about recruiting the new guys?" she asked.

She glanced around them. There was a table out on the patio making enough ruckus they had to be from the base.

"I was thinking about trying to recruit some guys from here. Like what about the table out there?"

Brian shook his head. "No. I know them. Those guys are active duty. Even if they were willing to use up their limited days of leave for production, the team could still get called up at any time. You want guys who just got out of the teams. They're available. They've got time on their hands and while transitioning out and back to civilian life they're going to want to prove that they've still got what it takes even though they're out."

A bubble of hope and joy rose inside her chest.

She turned to Alicia. "Your man is brilliant. You know that, right?"

Alicia frowned. "Shh. I don't need him getting cocky about it."

"Thanks, babe. You're always right there keeping me humble." He shook his head and let out a chuckle before he turned his attention back to Shelly. "I'll hook you up with a list of local guys who just got out, if it will help."

"Yes, it will help." She let out a breath, finally feeling

the weight lift and like she might have a future again. "I can't thank you enough."

"No thanks needed. Just don't ask me to fix you up again and we'll call it even."

"Done." She beamed.

It was an easy promise to make. Who needed a man when she could have a hit show instead?

4

Shelly realized the error in her plan pretty quickly. It was clear by the steady shaking of the heads of the three men standing in front of her.

She'd done everything right.

Waited for the bridal shower to get rolling and for the guys to get a couple of drinks in them before she'd approached, isolating them from their dates and the rest of the guests in a corner of the yard.

She set the idea up as a challenge they didn't want to miss to tempt them before giving the details.

When she presented the concept to them, Nick laughed out loud.

Zach had trouble swallowing his mouthful of beer before looking at her like she'd grown another head.

Clay glared at her, his jaw set as he delivered a definitive, "No."

"Hell, no," Zach elaborated.

"Good luck with it though," Nick added. The youngest of the bunch always was sweet and polite.

"But—"

"No," Clay repeated, the crease in his forehead above his icy stare deepening.

"You'd be paired up with your wives," she added quickly as incentive.

That had all three of them, even stone-faced Clay, breaking into a smile and then an outright laugh.

"Tasha? On the O-Course?" Clay let out a snort. "Might be worth saying yes just to see that."

Her hopes rose like a phoenix from the ashes.

"But no," Clay said, with a firm shake of his head.

"It would only be for—"

"No," all three said at once, cutting her off.

She let out a sigh. "All right. Thanks for listening."

They nodded and as she walked away, slow and in mourning over her career as it died before her very eyes, she heard them continue to chat about the ridiculous concept of their wives being on the show.

"Can you picture Tasha on her stomach in the sand, getting all dirty and sweaty for the Low Crawl?" Clay laughed.

Nick let out a chuckle. "Or Dani trying to get over the Dirty Name. She would give it two tries, fail and then stalk off mad."

"Gabby doesn't do anything fast unless it's running down the aisle at Home Depot to get the last item on sale on Black Friday," Zach added. "It would take her an hour to complete that course, minimum."

The three men continued to amuse themselves at the expense of her idea as she slinked off to the kitchen.

There was a case of some nice wine chilling in the fridge. She knew because she'd arranged for the delivery from a show sponsor.

She couldn't think of a better time to crack open one of those babies and drown her sorrows.

Apparently, she wasn't the only one with that same idea. The women were already there, wine glasses in hand as they chatted, unaware their men were disparaging their athletic abilities just outside.

"Shelly. Hi. Come join us," Gabby said in her usual welcoming tone. "I'd offer you something to eat but Tasha made me move the charcuterie board to the other room so it wouldn't tempt her."

"I'm sorry. But I could barely zip my dress today." Tasha shook her head. "Gain a couple of pounds and it settles right in my boobs."

"Oh, you poor thing." Dani rolled her eyes. "I'm sure Clay hates that your boobs are bigger."

"Wine?" Gabby asked, diffusing the sarcasm while reaching for an empty glass from the ones laid out in neat, Instagram-worthy rows on the counter by the open bottle.

That was part of the sponsorship deal. Shelly was to make sure they all posted pictures of the guests—and especially the shows' stars— enjoying the wine on social media. She'd have to make sure the cameraman had gotten some good footage of them all drinking it as well. Influencer marketing at its best.

"Yes, please. Thank you. I could use a drink." Shelly sighed as she took the glass Gabby offered.

"I know that tone. Men problems?" Tasha asked.

She laughed. "Kind of, but more executive producer problems."

Dani, who had worked beneath Joanne before she left New Millennia Media, groaned in commiseration. "I hear you on that."

"Anything we can do to help?" Gabby asked.

"Unless you can get your men to agree to shoot a sizzle reel for me, not really."

"A sizzle reel for what?" Dani asked, her producer ears perking up.

"For one of our shows?" Tasha asked.

Tasha had been in front of the camera for years as a morning talk show host. And in spite of the fact she was just weeks away from marrying the camera-adverse Clay, she was always willing to put in the extra work whenever NMM asked them to.

All three women were focused on Shelly, eagerly waiting for her to explain the concept for the show that their men had so quickly shot down.

Why hadn't she thought of this before? Brian and Alicia had been wrong.

Appealing to the competitive nature of three of the most alpha males she'd ever met, confident men who had nothing to prove to anyone, was the wrong tactic.

She needed to appeal to the women. Afterall, all three of the SEALs had appeared on reality shows not because they wanted to. Oh, no. They had most definitely *not* wanted to. But they all did it to help the careers of the women they loved.

These women.

Shelly drew in a breath and launched into her carefully worded presentation. "I came up with an idea for a new show. Teams of two, made up of one Navy SEAL and one civilian, would compete against each other in challenges based on the actual training the guys go through during BUD/S."

Dani nodded. "Sounds like a great concept to me. Right in New Millennia's wheelhouse. So what's the problem?"

"I've had no problem finding SEALs for five of the teams. And I have a casting call scheduled for the five civilians. That will cover five of the eight teams competing. The issue is that Joanne wanted the final three to be made of up celebrity teams."

Shelly threw that word—celebrity—out there to woo the women. Stroke their egos a bit. Remind them that NMM was responsible for them having a million plus followers on Instagram.

"You three, to be exact" Shelly elaborated. "With Clay, Zach and Nick as your partners."

She watched for a reaction.

Tasha's eyes lit up. "I love it."

"I'm not sure how good I'll be but I'd be willing to

give it a shot." Gabby nodded.

The only hold out looked like it would be Dani. She'd quit NMM and hadn't looked back. Not since *Cold Feet*, the bridal show—and the final project—she'd worked on with Nick.

Dani's gaze settled on Shelly's. "Joanne's going to be very unhappy if you don't get us to do the show."

"Yes," Shelly admitted.

There was no use lying to Dani about the reality of the situation. Dani knew Joanne. She knew what working for NMM was like from personal experience. It was one reason she now worked somewhere else.

Dani sighed. "All right. Nick and I will do it. For you, Shell. Not for Joanne or New Millennia."

Shelly couldn't help the uncontrollable smile that gripped her. "Thank you so much." But they weren't exactly in the clear yet. "There's just one problem…"

As the three women watched and waited Shelly drew in a breath and then let the truth spill out.

"The guys already told me no. Emphatically," she added.

Tasha sniffed out a laugh. "You leave the guys to us."

"Yeah. I have my ways of convincing Zach." Gabby grinned mischievously.

Dani frowned. "Knowing how competitive the guys are, I'm surprised they said no. I figured it would be right up their alley."

"Right? That's what I thought." Shelly nodded in agreement.

"Don't worry. Nick'll do it," Dani assured her. "He'll do anything for me."

Tasha nodded. "Then Clay will have to do it too, to save face."

"We got you. Don't worry about a thing," Gabby agreed.

With that assurance, Shelly breathed freely for the first time in days. "Thank you so much."

"Thank *you*. I'm looking forward to it." Tasha smiled.

"You mean you're looking forward to the ratings boost for *Hot House* this show will bring," Dani guessed.

"Yeah. There's that." Tasha raised her glass. "To—what's the name of the new show?"

Shelly felt shy admitting it, but she'd come up with a name and hadn't had the nerve to pitch it to Joanne yet.

"I'm thinking Under Pressure? Like that old song. I thought it was fitting." Shelly shrugged.

"Okay." Tasha nodded and glanced around with her glass lifted high. "Here's to *Under Pressure*."

The others raised their glasses and Shelly's hopes and dreams for this show and for her career—hope she'd been afraid to set free until now—took wings and soared.

"Shelly!" Clay's voice came from behind her, deep, firm and so loud it made her jump.

Uh oh. Did he know she'd gone behind his back to recruit Tasha and the other women after the men had already said no?

"Um, yeah?" She turned slowly and with undeniable

fear in her gut, found Clay with her gaze. He was stalking angrily toward the road.

Holy shit. Was he leaving the party because of her?

Tasha's laugh had Shelly turning back.

"He's calling the dog." Tasha smiled. "He found her as a puppy on the beach… like a seashell. So he named her Shelly."

Shelly blew out a breath, relieved though her heart continued to pound as she recovered. "Oh. Funny coincidence."

Dani shot her a knowing glance, as if she could guess what Shelly had been thinking. "Funny, indeed."

Shelly raised her glass to take another sip and realized it was empty. "Um, is there more of that wine?"

She was going to need it. This project was already driving her to drink.

5

Leaning against the bumper of his parked Jeep, Stefan watched his five teammates walking toward him from the two vehicles they'd just arrived in.

He'd gone down to the beach early to warm-up and stretch before he kicked their butts on the course. Apparently, his teammates had taken the time to enjoy a leisurely breakfast instead.

When they got close enough to hear, he asked, "Are you finally ready to do this?"

"No." Danny scowled.

Stefan drew back. "What do you mean, *no*? We already delayed this thing because the candidates were on the course yesterday."

Begrudgingly, Stefan had given in and admitted that SEAL candidates in the middle of BUD/S training had to take precedence over the bet between him and his teammates regarding his nickname.

But there were no candidates scheduled to test here this morning. He'd checked. So the bet was back on. Time to settle this thing.

"There's a bunch of people and a camera crew over there." Danny lifted his chin in the direction of where there was indeed an assembly of people, most looking completely out of place.

Men. Women. Lights. Equipment. Vans.

Normally, he'd be curious. Today, he just wanted to get this thing over with. His future identity hung in the balance.

"So what?" Stefan shrugged, looking back to his teammates. "Ignore them."

"What if they're filming a recruiting commercial or something?" Eric asked.

"You're just afraid I'll beat you," Stefan accused after a derogatory huff.

"No. We're afraid command is going to be pissed if we go busting in there and ruin their shoot. Especially if they are some high-dollar ad company from LA the Navy is paying to be here," Mason added.

Stefan sighed. "Fine. I'll go over there and ask them who they are and why they're here. But if they're not filming some kind of official thing for the Navy, they're the ones who can wait for us. Active-duty teams take priority over film crews, or whoever they are, when it comes to use of our own base equipment."

"All right. You go for it." Wyatt folded his arms over his chest, indicating he'd be there waiting and probably hoping Stefan's plans got shot down by these interlopers.

"But, hey, if that sexy Sierra Cox is over there with her film crew, give us a signal. I wanna meet her." Ty grinned.

There were mumbles of agreement on that point, all of which Stefan ignored as he spun around to stalk across the sand toward the group.

He seriously doubted Sierra Cox was here. Although, he was pretty sure he had heard a rumor she was dating a retired team guy, so who knew? Crazier things had happened. This was California, land of the stars.

Reaching the group, he saw Sierra Cox was not there, but there was a whole lot of other insanely hot females. So many he had to wonder if this was a shoot for *Love Island* or something.

What blew that theory were the males in the group. All had the feel of team guys about them. More than that, all of them were decked out in PT gear with big bold letters that spelled out NAVY emblazoned across the chest.

What the hell was going on?

Was this a special *Love Island: Coronado* and they'd cast SEALs? And why the hell did he keep thinking about *Love Island*? Damn his sister for making him binge watch a whole season of that dumbass show the last time he was home visiting for the holidays.

The other people on the beach were definitely a camera crew. But what were they here shooting?

If this were a shoot for a Navy ad, what was the recruitment message supposed to be?

Judging by this odd mix of sailors and hot chicks who could all fit into the cast of *America's Next Top Model*, the new recruiting slogan might well be something like *Join the Navy and get all the hot girls*.

"I'm sorry. I'm going to have to ask you to clear the beach. We've got a permit to film here this morning."

At the sound of the voice behind him, Stefan raised his brows in a mix of shock and defiance at being ejected from what he considered his territory.

Turning, he was about to tell her he didn't give a shit about her permit, when he found himself face-to-face with one of the aforementioned hot chicks.

This one a blonde that would look far better, and less out of place here, in a bikini instead of the business attire she wore.

Blue eyes met his as she flashed him a bleach-white smile that was most likely meant to soften the blow of her telling him he had to leave.

She was tall with mile-long legs but she was curvy in all the right places. The kind of woman he'd probably flirt with had they met one night at McP's Pub and he was in the mood for female company.

The one unattractive thing about her was, judging by her clipboard and her attitude, she thought she was in charge here.

She also obviously thought that she could tell him what to do. There she was wrong.

He folded his arms. "This equipment is base property."

She nodded. "Which is why I obtained permission from the base to be here."

"Why?" he asked.

A frown marred her formerly smooth brow. "Because we need to film the obstacle course."

"Why?" he repeated, hoping to get a better answer this time.

Her sweet as pie demeanor cracked a bit more as she frowned deeper. "I'm sorry if it's an inconvenience for you, but—"

He snorted at her non-answer as a dark-haired man, who was maybe in his forties, walked up and said, "Shelly."

Shelly. At least now he had a name to go with the hot but evasive woman standing between him and his goal—that goal being his kicking his teammates' asses on the O-Course.

At the interruption, she turned to face the newcomer.

She let out a loud exhale. "Clay. Thank God. You were so late I was worried you weren't coming. Where's Tasha?"

"That's what I need to talk to you about. In *private*." The guy she'd called Clay glanced briefly at Stefan before focusing back on her.

If they wanted privacy, they probably shouldn't be meeting here and now. But Stefan was fine with taking a step back if it would move things along a little faster.

He turned and glanced at his teammates. Raising both hands palms up, he shrugged and hoped that told them he didn't know any more than they did yet. But he wasn't giving up.

When he turned back he found his nemesis had been pulled a few yards away where she was in deep in what looked to be a serious discussion with the guy who, like a lot of the others with the group, had the look of a SEAL about him.

Judging by the body language and the expression on the face of the blonde—Shelly—things were not well in Hollywoodtown.

A couple of long minutes later, the guy left and she turned. He took the opportunity to move in before she escaped into a conversation with someone else.

Trotting to where she stood looking distraught, he said, "Hey, can we finish our conversation?"

Her gaze came back to him as she drew in a big breath and let it out.

"I'm sorry. What did you want again?" she asked.

With all the color drained out of her face except for two pink spots on her cheeks, the look made her appear even more like a porcelain doll.

She looked flustered. That made him wonder why.

"Problem?" he asked, hating that he actually cared.

"You could say that." She let out a huff. "One of the teams just dropped out."

"Teams?" He shook his head, confused.

After a few seconds of hesitation, she drew in a breath and said, "We're shooting a new show. A competition between eight teams."

"A show," he repeated. "So this isn't some sort of ad for the Navy?"

She frowned. "An ad for the Navy? No. We produce reality shows."

That was a relief. "All right. So look, it sounds like you're going to be here all day with your competition. My teammates and I only need the course for like forty-five minutes, so can we jump ahead of you?"

"Sure. Go ahead." She threw her hands up. "You might as well. There might not be a shoot anymore anyway."

"Why?" he asked, again kicking himself mentally for not just signaling the guys and getting their runs in now before she changed her mind.

"Because now we only have seven teams instead of eight."

"And that's a problem because?"

She leveled a wide-eyed glare on him. "Because besides the fact the executive producer really wanted Clay and Tasha and they just dropped out, I set up the competition and elimination schedule for the whole season for eight teams."

"So change it to seven," he suggested.

"I can't just change it. It'll alter the whole schedule for the rest of the episodes. What if one of the Sweet Sixteen teams dropped out? Or worse, one of the Final Four. That would totally mess up the brackets."

A woman who looked like a model and spoke like a bookie during March Madness? "You know college basketball?" he asked, intrigued.

"Of course, I know college basketball. I graduated from UCLA." She scowled at him. "I need to go deal with this, so I guess the course is yours. For now," she added the warning. "Please be done within the hour. The crew is costing us a lot of money to just have them standing around."

He blew out a breath. "I don't need an hour. *I'll* be done in six minutes. The other five guys might take a little bit longer but yeah, we'll be out of your way in an hour."

"Thank you," she said, without much warmth of actual gratitude in her tone, before she spun away.

As he watched her leave in a huff, trying and failing to stomp away in the soft sand, he had to smile.

She was a spitfire. Annoying. Superior. But a firecracker, none-the-less.

"You're welcome," he said at her back, knowing she probably wouldn't hear.

Then it was time to focus on the competition at hand.

She might have whatever odd eight-team bracket she'd set up to deal with, but he had his reputation on the line. And he'd be damned if his SEAL legacy, which would follow him past retirement and until the day he died, would be tied to his mother's pierogi and not his many and varied qualifications as a skilled operator.

Pivoting in the sand, he waved them over as he yelled, "We're up. Who wants to be first?"

He had every intention of going last and beating every one of their times.

6

"What's up?" Jerry, the cameraman, met Shelly, stopping her in her path as she walked toward the group where she saw Clay huddled with Nick, Dani, Zach and Gabby."

Shelly dragged her gaze back to Jerry. "Clay told me they just found out Tasha is pregnant. Like this morning when she took a test. So she's pulling them out of the show."

"How pregnant can she be?" Jerry asked. "A month? She wasn't even showing at the shower. It won't matter for this. It's just a sizzle reel."

"Yeah, but what if it gets picked up and we have to start production while she's huge?" Shelly shook her head. "Clay's having nothing of it anyway. He told me in no uncertain terms he is not letting her run the obstacle course, or do any of the other challenges we have planned, while she's pregnant."

"So what do you want to do?" Jerry asked.

"I don't know yet." She needed time to think.

Unfortunately, with all the crew standing around while on the clock, she couldn't take long. She figured she had the amount of time it took the guys who were currently on the obstacle course to gather her thoughts, then they needed to get to work.

She glanced over at them now. One was already running the course while the others cheered him on.

"We can shoot the sizzle reel without them and worry about finding a replacement team if the show gets picked up," Jerry suggested.

If. That little two letter word seemed very big and frightening in relation to the future of *Under Pressure*.

Her show, like countless others, might never get the green light. That was the reality of this business.

"It's not ideal, and not what Joanne wanted, but we might have to do just that," she agreed, her gaze still on the team running the course.

They should probably all be watching these SEALs run the obstacles—the crew especially—so they could plan how best to shoot the teams when it was their time on the course.

"Hey. You okay?" Dani asked as she walked up to Shelly.

"As good as can be expected." Shelly sighed and turned to fully face Dani. She glanced over at Clay, then back to Dani. "I assume you heard."

"The good news?" Dani smiled knowingly.

Shelly let out a short laugh. "I am happy for them."

"But now you have to replace them and Joanne wanted a high profile team," Dani completed Shelly's unspoken thought.

"Yup." She drew in a breath, her lips pressed tight.

Her whole body felt tight. Like a rubber band about to snap.

Dani cringed. "Good luck."

"Thanks," she answered without feeling.

"I'm going to head back over," Dani hooked a thumb toward the group. "Maybe, together, we can come up with a solution for you."

"That would be great. Thank you."

As Dani moved away, Shelly was having trouble holding on to much hope.

The crew, obviously looking for instructions, had already started to gather around her as she'd been speaking to Dani.

The sound guy said, "If you're looking for some high profile people to be a team, what about Sierra Cox and her fiancé? I mean you showed us the video of that SEAL running the course that gave you the idea for the show in the first place."

The guy manning camera two shook his head. "I read Sierra is in Australia filming a movie."

Shelly frowned. "I thought she was in New Zealand."

The cameraman shrugged. "Same thing."

It really wasn't, but it didn't matter as far as this situation anyway. They couldn't afford Sierra Cox, even if she were in the country and available and willing to do the show. Shelly doubted the Academy Award winner would be interested in this project *or* work for scale when she was pulling in multi-millions for every film.

"What about one of these guys?" Jerry asked, the camera on his shoulder again as he watched the action on the course through the lens.

"They do look pretty good out there," the sound guy agreed.

She turned to follow his gaze. It didn't matter how good they looked, because Joanne had her heart set on Clay and Tasha. And what Joanne wanted she was used to getting.

Pregnant. Jeez. What were the odds? Although Tasha had said she'd gained a few pounds and her boobs were bigger. Not being a mother, Shelly had completely missed that clue.

Getting a glance at Clay where he still spoke with Nick, Zach, and Gabby, she had to admit with how hot these guys were, it was more of a surprise there hadn't been a NMM baby long before this.

These couples were going to make gorgeous babies. Through her misery about *Under Pressure* possibly dying before it even began, another idea struck her.

They could build a show around Tasha's pregnancy.

Hot House Baby. *Baby in the House*. *Hot Babies*…no. That last one kind of sucked.

It didn't matter. She'd think of a good title. Then she'd pitch it to Joanne, at the same time she told her boss Clay had put his foot down and wasn't going to let Tasha do anything as physical as this competition when she was carrying his baby.

Hopefully the idea of a ratings-grabbing baby, not to mention the new viewership and sponsors a baby would attract, would distract Joanne from the fact they'd lost Clay and Tasha for this show.

Until then, she needed to get this sizzle reel shot, edited and to Joanne before the end of the week. Then, if—when—a network greenlit the show, she'd come up with an eighth team. All she needed was another SEAL and another civilian.

Brian had performed some magic, hooking her up with a short list of SEALs who had recently gotten out of the Navy but still lived in the area. She'd contacted them and once they heard they'd be getting paid they were totally into it.

She would have to go back to Brian and ask for one or two more SEAL recommendations and then revisit some of the women they'd considered during the open call.

But that was a problem for later. Today, they needed to get moving.

She eyed the SEALs gathered around the start of the course watching one of their own systematically work his way through the obstacles. He was currently climbing a high wall like he was born to do it.

"Jerry. Can you get these guys on tape?" she asked as she watched the impressive performance.

"On it." The camera already on his shoulder, he moved closer to the action.

"Me too?" the sound guy asked.

The image of the edited footage of the SEALs dominating the obstacle course on the opening of the teaser reel coalesced in her mind.

"Yeah. Camera two as well."

He nodded and moved off while she spun and searched for the new guy who'd just started and was acting today as her assistant. She hoped he was on top of things.

"Jonas!" she called. When he turned and trotted closer, she asked, "Any chance you've got some blank release forms with you?"

"Got 'em in the van." He tipped his head toward where they'd parked the production vehicles.

"Can you get all of those SEALs over there to each sign a release? That way we can use what we capture today for B-roll. It'll be good filler."

And she might need filler, and lots of it, now that one of her teams had dropped out.

"You got it." Jonas took off at a run, reminding her of herself her first week on the job. Back when she was new and eager and full of energy and dreams.

That feeling of life and her career being bright, shiny and new was long gone.

Today, she was in charge and she felt the weight of that in every fiber of her being.

Joanne had shown huge confidence in her, an associate producer, by letting her run this shoot.

Of course, Joanne hadn't had much choice. She'd had to have faith in Shelly. This shoot had been thrown together so last minute that all the usual directors and producers were already tied up on other sets, working on other projects.

No matter how she'd gotten put in charge for the day, Shelly couldn't let Joanne down. This was her opportunity to prove herself and she wasn't going to screw it up.

Baby, or no baby, her future depended on making this happen.

While she racked her brain on how to do that, the noise from the group of SEALs increased, drawing her attention.

Between the heckling and cheering, she got the idea that these guys were in competition against each other.

This was exactly the spirit she wanted for the show. Hot competition. Hot heads. Jubilant winners. Angry losers.

Male pride at its best and most dramatic.

She glanced at the teams she'd recruited for today. The women were milling around, sipping on water bottles and chatting with each other. But the eyes of every male cast member were glued to the course and the SEALs running it.

It was as if they were all chomping at the bit to get on it themselves. To prove to themselves and everyone else that they still had what it took.

Maybe that was her answer. It would up the competition factor to pit the seven former SEALs against one who was still on active duty.

There'd have to be some sort of rivalry between them, right? The old guard against the new. The past versus the present. It just might be enough of a conflict to appease Joanne as well as the viewers.

And with that thought, she started to watch the competition playing out before her more closely.

Whoever won among these six men might also win himself a contract and a spot on the next hit show.

The bubble of excitement was back. And this time she wasn't going to let anybody or anything deflate it.

7

"Emergency meeting," Lucy said as she walked past Shelly's desk.

Shelly whipped up her gaze as Lucy walked by. "What? Why? With who?"

Lucy paused and shook her head. "Your guess is as good as mine. All I know is Joanne's car just pulled up."

Joanne? Here. Now? It was too soon.

She thought she'd have until the end of the week to get the sizzle reel done. She was to present it at their regularly scheduled weekly meeting on Friday.

It was only Tuesday. What was Joanne doing here now? And what was this meeting about?

In a panic, she looked desperately to Lucy for answers. "You don't know why she's here?" Shelly asked.

Lucy was from the main office in Burbank. She was only in San Diego for a few weeks working on a project. She must have some insight about what was going on up there that would send Joanne down here days ahead of schedule.

The woman shrugged. "I guess we'll know soon enough."

"Yeah. I guess." Her heart pounding, she looked helplessly at her computer screen.

The cut was still raw. Rough. Incomplete. Nothing she'd want to show anyone yet. Particularly not the executive producer.

She'd show Joanne if the woman insisted, but she really didn't want to. Dammit.

The internal office message that slid across her computer screen confirmed Lucy's information.

Meeting room in five minutes.

Five minutes. There was nothing she could accomplish in that short of a time. Reconciling herself to that fact she grabbed her laptop and slunk to the meeting room.

She figured she might as well get a good seat at the table for the shitshow that her presentation was about to become if indeed *Under Pressure* was why Joanne was here.

Joanne blew into the room after everyone was already seated. There was an energy about her today, over and above the usual workaholic verve. Shelly tried to judge if the kinetic force radiating from the woman was good or bad.

But as Lucy had said, they'd know soon enough.

"Brandon from *Bed & Breakfast with Brandon and*

Brittany has been canceled," Joanne announced with a barely controlled smile.

"The show's been canceled?" Lucy asked.

"*Brandon's* been canceled. He got caught with his pants down, literally," Joanne explained with a glee the situation didn't warrant. "We can thank today's cancel culture that the show has been cut from the network's schedule immediately."

Every person at the table, except for Shelly, had their cell phones out. No doubt they were all Googling, looking for digital evidence of what Joanne had just told them.

"Holy shit," Jonas breathed. "Social media is tearing him apart for cheating on her." He glanced up. "And it gets worse than that."

"How can it get worse?" Shelly asked.

Lucy, cell in hand, jumped in. "It looks like Brittany defended him and though I suppose I should respect her for sticking by her man and all that, social media really latched onto that."

"It was like throwing gasoline on a fire. Half the audience supported her decision. The other half condemned her," Jonas continued.

"What does this mean for us?" One of the social media coordinators asked.

It was a good question. B&B wasn't one of New Millennia Media's shows. As their competition for ratings, the fate of the show was of interest, but B&B's downfall didn't directly affect them at NMM.

"It means there is now a big hole in The Reality

Network's line-up. TRN isn't even airing the rest of the season's episodes that are already in the can. That hole in their schedule is one I want us to fill." Joanne redirected her focus to Shelly. "And I want to fill it with the SEAL competition you pitched to me."

Shelly's eyes flew wide. "*Under Pressure?*"

Joanne nodded. "I called the executives over there the minute I heard. They greenlit ten episodes of *Under Pressure*. And they need them now."

"Now? We—how?" Shelly stuttered.

"We only need to have episode one to them to air next week. We'll just deliver the rest as we get them edited. We've worked on a tight deadline before."

"Yes, but—" Shelly tried to protest as Joanne turned to Lucy, who was apparently jumping in to work as the social media coordinator for this last minute project.

"We've got the bios and the headshots for the cast already, so there's basic content for all the contestants to work with. Can you throw together a website for the show today?" Joanne asked.

"Yes, ma'am." Lucy nodded with a smile of confidence that Shelly only wished she felt.

Joanne moved her attention to the head of the editing department. "We've got the footage we shot for the sizzle reel. I think from that we can create the intro show pretty easily."

Editing nodded. "I agree."

Joanne finally brought her focus back to Shelly. "You

just need to schedule the challenges and start filming for the rest of the episodes."

Just. Like it was going to be easy. Shelly sat, speechless.

Meanwhile, the moving train that was Joanne continued to barrel down the tracks. "We have to move on this quickly, people. We've been handed an opportunity. Let's not screw it up. That's it. Go. Make me a show."

The room emptied out, except for Jonas and Shelly and Joanne. Shelly's assistant was probably waiting for her to tell him what to do to help her. Meanwhile, she still had the task of breaking the bad news to Joanne about Clay and Tasha dropping out.

And she'd better get on that fast. Joanne was already heading for the doorway.

Shelly scrambled, her chair leg getting stuck on the carpet as she tried to shove away from the table to chase after Joanne.

Finally free, she stumbled and had to struggle to remain upright as she said, "Joanne!"

The woman turned, one brow cocked up.

"Tasha is pregnant." She hadn't meant to blurt it out quite like that. Too late now.

Both of Joanne's brows rose higher. "Really? That's good news. We'll have to plan for next season's *Hot House* to feature a nursery renovation."

"Yeah, I was thinking something along those lines—" Shelly stopped, seeing Joanne's mind was already elsewhere, as the woman herself would soon be if her slight shift in weight to her forward foot was any indication. "Clay pulled them out of *Under Pressure*. He won't let her compete pregnant. We're short one team."

Joanne's weight and her glance both shifted back toward the meeting room and Shelly. "So get another team."

"Oh, okay. I can do that. I was thinking maybe an active—"

Joanna shook her head. "I don't care. Use your judgement. You know what I want by now."

"Yes. I do. Okay. Thanks."

Joanne was headed for the editing room by the time Shelly called out her thanks and finally controlled her babbling.

"So who do you want?" Jonas asked.

She'd forgotten he was still there. "Let's take a look at what we shot of those SEALs who were on the obstacle course. The ones I had you get releases from."

"Okay." He nodded, following her to her desk. "One guy was really good. He beat all the others' times."

"Then we'll call him," she agreed.

"Actually, we might want to call his command first. My brother's in the Navy. The guy wouldn't be able to agree until he gets permission from his command."

She glanced at her assistant, impressed. "Good to know. Can you handle that?"

"Sure can."

"Great." That was one thing off her plate. Now she could concentrate on getting the best female counterpart.

It didn't matter which SEAL Jonas got. They were all in amazing shape. They'd look great on camera. And the faster their choice was, the more likely he would spur the other contestants into being more competitive, which made good television.

"As long as it's not that guy I had that fight with. The one who refused to sign," she added as she sat and pulled out the stack of releases from her file to hand to him.

Remembering the argument she'd gotten into with the SEAL who'd refused to sign the release had her blood pressure rising all over again.

She'd tried to explain to him how they'd have to blur out his face in every shot he was in if he didn't sign, but he didn't seem to care.

Selfish ass.

All his friends were thrilled. They all wanted to know more about the show so they could make sure to watch for it.

But not Mister Obnoxious.

She glanced up and saw the strange expression on Jonas's face. "He was the fastest one."

Shelly let out a snort. Having the obnoxious one on set would make her already difficult job harder. "Who was the second best?"

"The second best?" He raised his brows.

"Yeah. Do you know?" she asked.

He flipped through the stack of release forms in his hand before he nodded. "Ty Hogan came in second."

"Which one was he?" she asked pawing through her memory of that action filled day.

"About thirty. Dark hair. Green eyes. The other guys called him Flirt."

"Yes. I remember him. The one with the dimples. Perfect. Get him."

The camera would love him. The females on the set sure did.

Jonas looked less impressed with her choice but said, "Okay. If that's what you want."

"Yes. That's exactly what I want," she said definitively.

What was the difference between running the obstacle course in six minutes or seven minutes or whatever to the viewing public?

Besides, only an insane person would willingly choose to work with—enter into a contract with—the man who refused to even sign a simple consent form.

From that first moment she'd laid eyes on the hard-headed, hard-bodied man she knew he was trouble. That was proven when he'd muscled his way onto that obstacle course. When he'd demanded he go first even though they had permission to film there and were clearly set up to begin.

Karma was real. Because of all his faults, his behavior, his actions, that obnoxious SEAL had just lost himself an amazing opportunity.

The privilege, and the money that came with being on

Under Pressure, would now pass to his teammate. A teammate who was slower than he had been.

That would probably drive him crazy. Good. With a smile Shelly turned back to her computer screen. She had work to do.

Going through pictures and profiles of hot women to find one more for the show's team was probably a task Jonas would have enjoyed. And she would have gladly given it to him, but it seemed he knew more about military protocol than she did.

He was clearly more valuable dealing with that aspect. She'd just whip through these applicants. It wouldn't be hard. Today she was going to make one woman who'd been devastated at the thought she'd been passed over for the show very happy.

Shelly couldn't understand that desperation to be on camera herself. To be internet famous. To have your life play out in public.

Even after all her research for the show and knowing the horrors of SEAL training, she'd still rather go through BUD/S Hell Week than be in front of the camera for one of the reality shows produced by the company she'd hung her career on—dedicated her life to—but that was just her.

Thankfully, there were plenty of people lining up for a spot.

She was currently scrolling through those people when Jonas rushed over.

"Joanne wants you." His breathlessly gasped message had her swiveling her desk chair to face him.

"Okay…" She frowned, concerned. His tightly pressed lips and lifted brows didn't bode well. "What's wrong?"

"You'd just better come and talk to her yourself." Jonas's grim countenance was scaring her.

Was the footage they'd been counting on editing into the first show that bad that Joanne decided they couldn't use it? Or, worse, was it missing completely? Deleted by accident or something equally horrifying.

Anguished at the possibilities, she bolted from the chair.

Pushing past Jonas, she rushed out of her door and then realized she wasn't sure where Joanne was. Only that she wasn't here.

She spun to look back at Jonas, only to find him hot on her heels.

"Where is she?" she asked, as she started walking again toward the other side of the office.

"Editing," he supplied, keeping pace with her.

With a destination, she strode faster, making a beeline to the closed door of the room where the editors worked. Busting through the doorway, she swept the room with her gaze.

The editor was seated as Joanne stood over her shoulder. Both were focused on the screen until Joanne pivoted to glance back.

Her smile as she looked at Shelly didn't make sense. It

wasn't a friendly, welcoming smile. Or even a forced, fake smile.

It was the self-satisfied smile of someone who had solidified a scheme. The smile of the Joker as he birthed a plot to beat Batman. The Grinch as he envisioned his evil plan against Whoville.

And Joanne was aiming that smile at Shelly. A straight shot. She felt the direct hit.

"You asked for me?" she managed to ask, her heart thundering so hard it made her light-headed.

"Yes, I did." The smile spread, making Joanne look even more menacing than before.

She resisted the urge to take a step backward.

"I saw what you filmed yesterday. The teams on the O-Course for B-roll."

The O-Course. Ever since Joanne had started dating a SEAL, she'd begun to sound like one.

"Okay." Shelly nodded, waiting.

"We found our eighth team."

"We did? Okay. Which guy?" Relieved that it was just that Joanne had found a SEAL that tickled her fancy, Shelly took a step closer to the monitor.

"Him." Joanne tapped one manicured nail on the display.

Shelly's hopes sank as the SEAL she singled out was the thorn in her side. Mister Obnoxious. The one SEAL who hadn't signed a release. The one the editor should have been blurring out.

She was about to explain the difficulty with Joanne's

decision when Joanne turned back to her and said, "And you."

Shelly frowned. "Excuse me?"

"You and him. That's our eighth team."

Her eyes widened. "Me? But I have a whole folder on my computer filled with beautiful—"

Joanne brushed away that protest with the flick of a wrist. "Don't sell yourself short. You're gorgeous."

"But I'm in production. I'm not in front of the camera—"

"You are now. Welcome to the cast." Joanne shot her that evil impish smile again.

"Why?" she asked, losing this battle and completely at a loss of how to fight a force like Joanne Rossi.

"Watch for yourself." Joanne stepped to the side and said to the editor, "Show her."

Somehow the woman knew what Joanne meant. She tapped a few keys, rewound a bit of footage and suddenly Shelly was watching herself and the SEAL of her nightmares on the screen.

She had her hands on her hips and was saying something to him as he smirked at her, the unsigned release papers in his hands.

The angrier and more animated she became, the more amused he appeared until he outright laughed at her. That's when she stomped her foot and stormed away in an embarrassing career moment.

"I didn't know they got this on camera," she mumbled for a lack of anything else to say.

"You said get everything because we might be able to use it," Jonas offered, not so helpfully.

"I'm glad you did. It was a good instinct. This was exactly what I wanted between the couples on the teams. Fire. Passion," Joanne explained.

Passion. Couples? Her and him?

"Wait. What?" Shelly shook her head. "No."

"Yes," Joanne countered. "You're perfect."

"But you wanted a power couple like Clay—"

Joanne dismissed the objection with another flick of her gold and diamond encircled wrist. "We'll have Clay and Tasha visit. They can be guest judges or something. Ideally *after* she starts to show so we can tease the baby for the next season of *Hot House*. Sign this SEAL up today. I want him."

"That's going to be a problem. He refused to even sign a release for the B-roll," Shelly said, grasping onto to her one last objection that might actually work.

His stubbornness might be the thing that saved her from this Hell on Earth.

"We'll convince him," Joanne assured.

"But we don't even know his name," Shelly protested.

Joanne shook her head. "Easy enough to find out."

"I don't know how to even begin—"

Joanne raised a neatly shaped brow. "I'll take care of it."

"How?" Shelly asked.

"Let's just say I have an in at Coronado." That evil, scary, super villain smile was back.

Shelly had no doubt Joanne would get what she wanted. And she would end up as an unwilling participant in the show that had been her idea to begin with.

Maybe instead of *Under Pressure* she should have named it *Isn't it Ironic*. That seemed a more fitting song at the moment.

8

"Kowalski!" Wyatt bellowed from the doorway, loud enough it cut through the music pounding through Stefan's ear buds.

"What?" Stefan yelled back as he hung from the bar mid-chin-up.

"The lieutenant commander wants to see you."

"Now?" Stefan frowned.

"Now," Wyatt returned.

He sighed at the interruption to his gym time and dropped down to the ground, pulling the earpieces out of his ears after he landed.

Grabbing a towel, he wiped his face, then gathered his few things. This workout was obviously over. Just when he'd been getting into the zone, this.

A summons from command could be good or it could be bad.

Either way, the timing sucked. But he couldn't be too

annoyed since thanks to his kick ass performance on the O-course, no one could call him Pierogi anymore. The only thing that would have been worse would have been Wyatt bellowing that choice nickname across the gym for everyone inside to hear.

Before reporting to the head shed, Stefan gave the lieutenant commander who was interrupting him more deference than was due by changing into a clean dry T-shirt.

Was getting summoned at nineteen-hundred hours after he'd already been cut loose for the day really necessary? Stefan let out a huff of annoyance.

This had better be about something good. If it was an op, fine. Good. He was getting restless for some action. But if it was for some bullshit reason—he shook his head as just that thought had him getting annoyed before he even stepped through the doorway.

He stopped just inside the office. The sight of the blonde from the O-course seated at his LT's desk nailed his sneakers to the floor.

"Sir?" he asked, his gaze shooting between the woman, who'd twisted to glance at him, and his commander.

"Kowalski, have a seat."

He didn't want to sit. Especially not next to her.

Had she complained to his command because he hadn't signed her stupid form?

That was bullshit. He shouldn't be required to cooperate with any old stranger who wandered onto the obstacle course and claimed to have permission to be there.

With his lieutenant commander's eyes still focused on him, Stefan finally reached for the other chair.

He dragged it farther away from the female and sat on the very edge of the seat.

Stefan didn't have to wait long before his commander said, "I have a special assignment for you."

His ears perked up. Although this *assignment* couldn't be anything good. Command would never allow a civilian to be present for the discussion of an actual op.

"Sir?" Stefan prompted, staunchly ignoring the female and focusing solely on the officer seated opposite him.

"I'll let Miss Laurens explain."

Crap. Fighting a scowl, Stefan swiveled just his head to glance at her.

"I work for New Millennia Media."

"I know," he said flatly. That fact had been in the papers they'd shoved in front of his face on the course.

"We're producing a show. Eight two-man teams each comprised of one SEAL and one civilian will compete against each other."

"I know that too." It was what she'd told him as her reason for being on the course and in his way in the first place.

He even remembered being impressed with her college basketball bracket analogy as to why seven teams wouldn't work and she needed eight.

That was before she'd freaked out that he wouldn't

sign her form and had turned into a lunatic, stomping her feet and lecturing him in front of everyone within earshot.

With an expression that looked as if she'd tasted something bitter, she said, "We want you to be the SEAL for the eighth team."

That part was new.

"Why?" he asked.

"The competition is comprised of a series of challenges based on your SEAL training, that includes the obstacle course." Her gaze skipped away from his. In fact, she refused to meet his eyes when she said, "You were the fastest one on the obstacle course."

She was lying. Or at least holding something back.

"And? What else?"

Her gaze skittered to him briefly. "What do you mean?"

"Why do you want me?" he elaborated.

He'd asked around a bit after seeing her that morning. Curiosity, nothing more. He'd learned a bit about her and this show and the SEALs she'd assembled on the beach.

"From what I heard, you managed to secure a whole bunch of team guys who are already out," he continued. "I don't know much about making reality shows, but I know the Navy. It would be in your best interest to find one more guy who's already out of the service."

"The executive producer wants you," she said.

The way she still looked a bit uncomfortable led him to think maybe she wasn't on board with this producer's choice. He could use that.

"You do understand I'm active duty, right? That means if I get called up, I go. No matter what I'm doing at the time. Even your show." *Especially* the show.

"Actually, we've agreed to pull you from the team for the duration of the filming."

That blow had his head whipping to face the one ally he'd thought he had in this room. "Sir?"

His lieutenant commander nodded. "After speaking with Miss Rossi today about the benefits and recruitment potential this show would present, we decided your time over the next four weeks would be best spent working with Miss Laurens on this project."

Stefan felt physically sick to his stomach as he asked, "Is that an order, sir?"

The LT lifted one eyebrow. "Does it need to be?"

The indication was clear in the man's stare and his tone. Stefan was expected to be a team player. To do as told, no questions asked. Orders or no orders.

"No, sir." Swallowing hard, he sent this Miss Laurens, the bane of his existence, a glare. "I'd be happy to be on your show."

His words didn't match his tone. They didn't match his expression either, he was sure.

He was pissed at being forced to do something he didn't want to do. Enraged by the fear that rode him that if he didn't do as told it could affect his career. Future promotions. Assignments.

He nearly vibrated with anger and by her reaction, she

realized that too. There was no satisfaction or happiness in her. There was almost a look of fear.

Good. Fear he could handle. If she'd been gleeful over his loss and her victory, he didn't know what he would have done.

"Here is the contract for you to review. I had the legal department on base look it over and they're fine with it." His commander pushed a stack of stapled pages toward him.

He grabbed the papers and leaned back, half to get farther from her, half so he could lean his elbows on the arms of the chair and stop his hands from shaking.

It was hard to focus when he was this angry, so he mostly skimmed the document and only pretended to read and understand the legal jargon.

But one clause stood out, big and bold. He reread the paragraph. He'd be paid one thousand dollars for every episode in which he appeared. And there was a cash prize of fifty-thousand dollars to be split by the members of the winning team.

He could win this thing. He could use that money to put a down payment on a house. He could even take a few thousand out to send his parents to Poland.

Winning this whole thing wasn't out of the question. He was the best on the course. She'd said so herself. The question was who would he be partnered with?

If he could convince her, and the Navy as well, that it would be doubly good for recruitment if they paired him with a female sailor, his team would dominate the competition.

He'd seen the actresses and models they'd chosen for the other teams on the beach that morning. They looked real good but he doubted they'd get through day one of basic training, never mind BUD/S.

A little optimistic now, he glanced up. "Miss Laurens—"

"Please call me Shelly."

Noted, but he didn't call her anything as he asked, "Can I choose my own partner?"

"No." Again she looked more uncomfortable than the question warranted.

Intriguing, but he was too annoyed with her answer to think much more about it.

"Who will I be partnered with?" he asked.

She paused for what felt like a long time. Finally she glanced first at the commander and then at him before saying, "Me."

What the hell?

9

Shelly was out of the building and glaring against the sun as she tried to remember where she'd parked her car when she heard the sound of footsteps pounding the sidewalk behind her.

"Hey! Wait up."

Turning back, she saw her new SEAL partner jogging toward her. She drew in a breath and waited for him to get to her. During that time, she had the opportunity to plan her defense to the attack that was no doubt imminent.

The moment the muscle-bound man stopped in front of her, she said, "Look. I know you're not happy. I'm not happy either. Believe me."

His eyes pinned her with a glare. "So then do something about it. Aren't you in charge?"

She let out a very unladylike snort. "I wish. I'm about as in charge as you are. I had nothing to do with this. I'm an unwilling participant too."

When he still looked doubtful, she decided to put it in terms he'd understand.

"You have your commander. You have to do what he says. I have my executive producer. I do what she says or I could find myself out of a job and standing in the unemployment line. And good luck getting hired in this business once word spread I was let go."

He drew in and let out a breath, finally looking as if he believed her.

During that big breath, she managed to let her gaze drop to the muscles beneath his tight NAVY T-shirt for only a few seconds, so she considered that a win on her part.

"Okay. So what now?" he asked.

She wrestled her mind away from the awe and fantasies his hard body inspired and back to her bleak reality. "Now you wait for us to contact you once we start shooting the episodes."

"When will that be?" he asked.

She scoffed at the insanely unreasonable timeline this show was on. "Very soon."

If they didn't start within the next couple of days, she'd be up shit's creek without a paddle.

She'd heard that expression before and had never thought much about it. Now that she was neck deep in the proverbial shit, she understood it so much better.

"Soon? You can't be a little more precise than that?"

"At the moment, no. I still have to come up with the

episodes. Eight of them, all featuring riveting, ratings grabbing, camera worthy action."

"You don't have all that planned out already?" He frowned. His judgement was clear in his scowl.

"No," she spat out.

"I don't go into any op without extensive prior planning and preparation," he proclaimed haughtily.

La-de-da. Good for him. He had the whole Navy helping him with his planning and preparation. She had Jonas and his one week of experience in this business.

Unable to leave his judgement and passive aggressive insult go unchallenged, she narrowed her eyes and prepared to let it rip.

"Hey. I had a concept that was supposed to go from sizzle reel to green light to completed episodes over the course of months. I intended this to be a summer filler show for some network. And I would have been completely prepared if that had remained the timeline. Instead, I suddenly have a week to start delivering finished episodes to the network to be aired immediately."

He lifted one shoulder. "Shit happens sometimes. Good luck with it."

As he turned to leave, she blew out a breath. "Yeah. Thanks a lot. I appreciate it."

She wasn't able to control the sarcasm in her tone and didn't really care if he'd heard it until he pivoted back and glared at her with fire in his eyes.

"Hey, you can curb the attitude. You can't blame your

problems on me. Not my circus. Not my monkeys. *Not* my fault."

There he was wrong. This kind of was his fault. At least part of it. The part where Shelly got to produce and also be a cast member in this damn show with the impossible timeline.

If Stefan hadn't been such a spectacularly cocky asshole on that tape, Joanne would have never chosen him, and also her, to be the eighth team. The woman's love of SEALs was only surpassed by her craving for extreme drama on set in front of the cameras. The more the better.

But the rest, the tight deadline, *B&B* going down the toilet because Brandon couldn't keep his toolbelt buckled, that was not Stefan Kowalski's fault.

Shelly blew out a breath and controlled her anger and her frustration. As much as she hated to admit it, she was wrong to take things out on him.

Besides that, she didn't want to risk alienating this man. Like it or not, she needed him.

"I know it's not your fault. I'm sorry." She let out a sigh. "It'll be fine. I just have to get on Google and YouTube, search Navy SEALs and pick a bunch of training thingies you guys go through that we can adapt for the show fast and cheap."

His eyes widened for a second. "So, uh, that's what you're doing? Choosing the actual challenges for the show?"

She nodded. "Yup. It's going to be an all-nighter, but it

won't be my first in this job. And my assistant said he would help me—"

"I could, uh, maybe help. You know since I did go through the training myself and all." He shrugged.

For the first time since she'd met him he seemed... humble. Helpful.

The pivot in his personality was disconcerting. She wasn't quite sure what to do with this change in him, or his offer.

The last person she wanted help from was him. But he was also probably the most qualified to give it to her.

Stefan's assistance would save her from having to bother Alicia and Brian for help, or having to impose even more on Nick or Zach, who'd had to be coerced by their wives into agreeing to do the show in the first place.

As she weighed the pros and the cons of accepting the cocky SEALs help he waited quietly, displaying uncharacteristic patience.

Finally, she let out a breath. "Okay. Thank you. If you could make a list of trainings you think could convert well into challenges for the show—and maybe a brief description of them—I'd appreciate it."

She dug into her bag, pulled out a slightly battered business card from the side pocket and handed it to him.

"My email address and my cell number are both on there."

He took it and grinned. "Okay. You got it."

She frowned, wondering why he looked so happy when what she'd just done was give him what equated to a homework assignment. Something she'd assumed he'd balk about.

Instead, he looked happy as a clam as he said, "I'll get this list to you tonight."

"Uh, okay. That'd be great. Thanks."

"No problem." Another grin and tip of his head and he ran off. Legit *ran* at like top speed in the opposite direction.

She shook her head at his burst of energy and unexplained glee. But she couldn't deal with his strange behavior now. She had a show to plan and not nearly enough time to do it.

As she dug out her car key, she realized this situation called for a take-out order of tacos. A big one.

She wasn't kidding when she'd told him it was going to be an all-nighter. And she'd think far better if she was well fed for it.

10

"Hey, sis."

"Two calls in one week. What's wrong?" Irina asked.

"Nothing is wrong."

"Are you going away on a big op?" she asked. "You *are* being sent to Ukraine, aren't you?"

"For the last time, no." And even if he were, he couldn't tell her. "I have a question."

"Okay. Mom hasn't told me what she wants for Mother's Day, if that's it."

"No, but yeah, keep me informed of that if she mentions anything. I uh, wanted to ask what you know about New Millennia Media?" He glanced down at the small white card between his fingers.

"That's easy. Nothing. Who are they?"

That's what he was hoping she could answer. But he'd done a bit of recon already himself.

"They produce a bunch of reality shows." He glanced at the computer on the desk in his room. "*Hot House. Trash to Treasure. Cold Feet*—"

"Oh my God. I love all those shows. They're my absolute favorite!" she squealed.

He pulled the cell farther from his ear to save what little hearing he had left after years of being exposed to explosions and weapons fire.

"I thought *Love Island* was your favorite." Which was why he'd been subjected to it for most of his visit home last time.

"It was, until *Cold Feet*. All of my friends and I got totally addicted to that show. When that hot security guard Nick caught Katia when she fainted—oh my God. I was a goner. And don't get me started on the *Trash to Treasure Wedding* show and Zach. His and Gabby's wedding was ahh-mazing." She practically sang the last word, as if he hadn't already figured out she was over the moon about these stupid shows.

"All right. So these shows are popular then."

"Uh, yeah. Do they have you like living in a bunker there on base? Do you not have the internet?"

"I have the internet. I just choose to use it for other things."

"Like what? Ew! Porn?" she asked.

"Jesus—No." At least not that he was going to admit to his little sister. Time to change the subject. "Is Mom or Dad around?"

"Nope."

He tempered his annoyance at her unhelpful answer. "Would you like to tell me where they are?"

"The butcher."

Easter. Of course.

In the midst of this reality show crap, he'd forgotten about the impending holiday. There'd be kielbasa and stuffed cabbage rolls on the table. Not to mention hard-boiled, decorated eggs. The centerpiece would be the molded lamb made from butter, useful since it would be eaten with the bread also served. Then there were the cakes—always more than one. A whole buffet of them, including his favorite, babka.

And now he was homesick and hungry.

He sighed. "All right. Tell them I called and I'll call again on Sunday."

"You better. It's Easter on Sunday."

"Yes. I know. Bye, Irina."

"Bye, brat." She disconnected and was gone before he had time to lay down his cell and stare at the reality show site on the screen in front of him.

The people who were on these shows were front and center on the website. Which meant he would be too. If he was going to give up his privacy, his anonymity, he was damn well going to make it worth his while.

Time to rig this competition in his favor and ensure that money landed in his pocket and no one else's.

She needed competitive events, huh? He'd give Shelly the list she'd asked for, all right. And on it would be the things he personally excelled at, starting with the O-course.

"Knock, knock."

He glanced up and saw Wyatt standing in his doorway.

"We're going out. You coming?"

"I can't. I'm busy."

"Busy doing what?" Wyatt frowned and moved closer.

Doing something he hadn't told his team about yet but was going to have to.

Stefan leaned the screen of his laptop down so Wyatt wouldn't see the browser. It still displayed the reality shows his sister was so enthralled with. The same shows his team would tease him about relentlessly forever if they saw him looking at them.

And what were they going to do when he was actually on one? He might have a chance since his show was based on SEAL training and not on decorating your house with garbage or wooing bridesmaids or whatever happened on those other shows.

It was tempting to try and keep the whole mess secret from his team but that was going to be impossible. They'd notice when he started missing meetings and trainings and—and this one was going to hurt if it happened—ops.

No man wanted to be left behind when his brothers went off into danger. And he might have to do exactly that. For a dumb show. Under his command's *implied orders*—for lack of a better term.

He drew in a breath and spun the chair to face Wyatt. I have to tell you—all of you—something."

"Oh, shit. What happened?"

"Nothing. Well, nothing bad. At least not *that* bad." Giving up trying to qualify this debacle and how he felt about it he said, "Command called me in."

Wyatt nodded. "Yeah. I know. I'm the one who found you at the gym and told you."

"Yeah. Well, remember when we were on the O-course and that film crew had you all sign releases?"

"Yes." Wyatt frowned, looking confused as to the connection between the commander's summons and the O-course.

"The production people were there to shoot a new competition based on SEAL training."

"Yeah. They told us that when we signed." Wyatt nodded.

Stefan drew in a breath. "Command wants me to be on this show. As one of the competitors."

"That's amazing."

He snorted out a laugh. "Is it?"

"Yes. What's the problem?" Wyatt frowned.

The problem was he didn't want to do it. The LT was forcing him to do it.

Those complaints made him sound like a whiny bitch. But his other objection didn't.

"If the team gets spun up, I won't be able to go. I have to stay here for the *show*." He wrinkled his nose while saying the last word.

"Who are the other competitors?" Wyatt sat on the edge of the other chair and leaned forward looking actually interested.

"From what I can tell, a bunch of separated and retired SEALs. The guys we saw there that morning on the course."

Wyatt rubbed his hands together. "So you're going to kick their asses, obviously."

"Yeah. Probably." Stefan hesitated. "And actually, one of the producers—the blonde running things that day at the O-course—said she needed help planning the competitions. I offered to help."

"Dude. You can design the competitions? Oh my God. You totally are going to kick ass."

"That's kind of what I was thinking too."

"Hey, we going or not?" Ty leaned in.

Wyatt glanced at Stefan. "You want help?"

He shook his head. "You guys are on your way out—"

"For this, we'll adapt." Wyatt glanced at Ty. "Change of plans. Pick up a couple of six packs. Order a couple of pizzas and get all the guys in here. We have an op to plan. The team's reputation depends on it."

Recovering from the surprise, Stefan smiled. They might tease each other and annoy each other, but when they worked as a team, nothing could stop them.

Next stop, victory!

11

The smell of leftover tacos hung in the air as the containers littered the coffee table in the conference room of the New Millennia Media San Diego office.

The white board on the left was ready for them to fill in their brilliant ideas. It was numbered neatly down one side in purple marker and Lucy's inhumanly neat handwriting, *Episode 1* through *Episode 10*.

The white board on the right was less pretty. In Shelly's scrawl written in black marker was the list Stefan Kowalski, her SEAL partner—like it or not—had sent her.

She stared at his choices for the challenges and shook her head. Her fish tacos sat like a rock in her stomach. The sinking feeling of looming failure weighed the greasy food down, making it feel even heavier in her belly.

Stefan had come up with the most boring list of challenges ever.

She turned from the list she'd just transcribed from the text he'd sent to her phone and turned back to her co-workers. From Lucy's expression she could tell she wasn't the only one realizing they were in trouble.

"A pull-up competition to see who can do the most chin-ups? A push-up competition. Running race. Timed swimming." Lucy shook her head. "I'm not seeing anything that is going to grab ratings."

"I know," Shelly agreed.

"He even managed to make a parachuting episode sound boring. Whichever person floats and lands closest to the big X on the ground wins? That's not exactly riveting competition," Lucy pointed out.

"Yeah." Jonas nodded. "Aside from the fact we could put all the girls in bikinis for the competitions on the beach, it is pretty lackluster as far as challenges go."

Shelly scowled at him. "Hey. No bikinis on the girls since I'm going to be one of them.

He cringed. "Sorry. I forgot."

She wished she could forget. It turned out, she couldn't no matter how hard she tried. Now, her only hope was to make sure the show didn't flop. The only thing more embarrassing than being in this show that was her idea would be if it was a failure.

"Bikinis or no bikinis, can we—"

"No bikinis," Shelly reiterated, cutting Lucy off mid-sentence.

Lucy nodded, then continued, "Can we please at least start calling them *women* instead of girls?"

"Women," Jonas repeated. "I agree. Sorry."

Shelly expelled a lungful of air. Being referred to as a *girl* was the least of her problems right now. This show was going to be a complete and utter flop. Career ending unless they did something to make it work.

She decided her cohorts in this brainstorming session needed a reminder of that fact. "We won't be calling the women anything if we present this list of challenges. We'll be canceled before we even air."

"So let's change it up. Our job is to make it more exciting. Right?" Jonas glanced from one to the other.

Shelly turned to the newbie, so full of hope and enthusiasm. She gave him a year, two maximum, before this job beat him into the ground and robbed him of his dreams like it was so rapidly doing to her.

"I'm open to suggestions," she told him.

"I do have one idea," he said, suddenly shy.

"No idea is a bad idea at this point." Lucy stood and moved to the third white board, pristine and waiting for their great ideas.

Jonas leaned forward with his forearms braced on his knees and said, "What if the girls—women, sorry—are the only ones who compete? The SEALs act as coaches and trainers, but they don't actually do the challenges. Only their teammates do."

Lucy nodded. "So the SEALs will still be competitive because, of course, they want their team to win, but there will be the added frustration factor because even as skilled and trained as the guys are, the only thing that counts is how good they can make their teammate. They'll be forced to sit on the sidelines while their partners represent them. I *like* it." Lucy's gaze shot to Shelly. "What do you think?"

She hated to admit it, but she would have liked the idea too, *if* she weren't one of those who was going to have to compete.

All she could envision was Stefan, the fastest SEAL on the beach, yelling at her to be faster, do better, for all the episodes. At least, that was all she could think about until she did a mental review of some of the challenges they would plan. The challenges she would now have to perform alone.

Her heart pounding at even the thought of parachuting, she decided she'd better work on getting rid of the idea for that deadly episode immediately.

"Shell. What do you think?" Lucy asked when she remained silent.

Shelly sighed and finally admitted, "It's a great idea."

And it would be good for the show. Sometimes that was all that mattered.

Jonas broke into a wide grin as Lucy wrote the idea on the board and they were on their way.

"Now to liven up some of these competitions," Lucy began. "What about all that stuff we've seen pictures of them doing during Hell Week? Carrying logs over their heads. Carrying boats over their head. There seems to be a lot of carrying."

"So much of Hell Week is about working as a team.

Like the log carry," Jonas pointed out. "We need things that can be done by a single person."

"True. It's always a bunch of them doing it together." Lucy nodded.

"There are a couple of individual things. Like drown-proofing," Jonas said.

"What's that?" Shelly asked, afraid she didn't want to know.

"They, uh, pretty much drown you. At least they come as close as they can without actually doing it."

Jonas seemed to know a hell of a lot about SEALs. At the moment, Shelly wished he didn't.

"And the point of that is?" she asked.

"To conquer any fear of water."

"That would not only give me fear. It'd give me nightmares." Lucy looked as horrified as Shelly felt at the idea.

"Well, it's also so you'll keep calm if and when you actually are in danger of drowning." Jonas shrugged.

Shelly shook her head. "I'm not letting them drown me. What else have you got?"

"Sugar cookies," he suggested.

That didn't sound so bad. She knew better than to assume so she asked, "What is it exactly?"

"You lay in the surf, which makes you get all covered with sand that sticks to you because you're wet. Like a sugar cookie."

She hated being wet—and sandy—but it was better

than being drowned. "Okay. That's a possibility. Although it doesn't sound all that exciting."

Jonas nodded. "Mm. True. We could do a combined sugar cookies, sit-up and push-up competition. Who can complete the reps fastest maybe? Or endurance—who can do the most before giving up."

Shelly scowled. "This is sounding all much more athletic than I anticipated."

"That's what makes it fun." Lucy grinned.

"For you, maybe." Shelly frowned.

"Okay, we'll pencil in sugar cookies," Lucy said, moving to write on the board while Shelly mentally kicked herself for even suggesting this show in the first place.

12

It wasn't quite an all nighter. They broke about one-thirty in the morning. Everyone went home to grab a few hours' sleep and a shower before the presentation the next morning.

Shelly walked through the door of the office just before eight-thirty the next morning, extra-large coffee in hand.

Since Joanne wouldn't care how late they'd worked, and since there was more work to do than time to do it, they had the meeting scheduled for nine.

They couldn't waste any time. They had to get the first episode tightened up and complete and to the network. Then they had to get filming the next nine.

It would take a miracle.

And speaking of miracles—Lucy had pulled off some magic and had the presentation in PowerPoint and already projected up on the screen by the time Shelly arrived in the conference room.

She stopped just inside the doorway and stared at the *Under Pressure* graphic on the wall. "Oh my God. Lucy, this looks great."

Leaning over the laptop running the presentation, Lucy accepted the compliment with a cautious smile. "Thanks. Let's hope everybody else thinks so."

She was no doubt talking about Joanne. And not just Joanne, but the network as well. So many people depending on them. Judging them.

Why was she in this business again? Fame? Nope. Not yet. Fortune? Definitely not at her level.

"Good. You're here early." Joanne strode into the room like a boss, glancing from Lucy to Shelly.

Lucy straightened up and snapped to attention. "Good morning, Joanne."

Joanne nodded in reply. She pulled out a chair at the table, sat, and leaned back as she waited for them to entertain her.

Shelly moved to the table and set down her laptop and file folders containing her life at the moment—everything she'd gathered to do with *Under Pressure*.

Jonas walked into the room, his eyes widening when he saw Joanne already seated and Shelly and Lucy both there.

His fear-filled gaze shot to Shelly. She lifted one shoulder.

With a look of trepidation, he glanced at the clock on

the wall, as if to confirm she was indeed twenty minutes early and it wasn't him who was late to the meeting.

Even so, he sidled silently along the wall and took a seat at the end of the table, out of Joanne's sightline.

Lucy looked as if she'd just realized she was still standing in the front of the room and slipped into a chair at the table. That left Shelly as the last one standing.

She moved to the laptop Lucy had left open and connected to the projector.

Clearing her throat, she reached to tap the key and prepared to begin.

"Episode one is the introduction of the cast members. We've got some great footage from the obstacle course where they first met each other and interacted throughout the day. We've got bios and headshots and we've already filmed all of them—"

Shelly stopped herself when she realized that two cast members were missing. Her and Stefan. She regrouped and corrected her initial statement.

"—almost all of them on camera introducing themselves. That should be enough to fill the first hour."

She'd have to pin Stefan down and get him to talk about himself. That should be real fun. *Not.*

Then, she had to do it herself too. Ugh.

As she pondered the upcoming horrors, Lucy leaned forward. "From what we have already for episode one, we'll be able to set up the characters for the season. The most competitive, the diva, the bitch, the flirt, and so on."

Lovely. Shelly wondered which one she'd be cast as.

"I've already started to build the site with features for each of the cast," Lucy continued.

When Lucy finally finished, Shelly said, "All right. Moving on to episode two. This will be the cast's arrival on San Clemente Island where they'll set up—by themselves—the tents they'll be staying in for the time they're there."

"We have permission and permits for San Clemente Island?" Joanne asked.

"Applied for it yesterday. Just waiting for approval," Jonas replied.

Joanne tipped her head in a nod. "Let me know if there's any problems with it," she said before turning her attention back to Shelly.

"Episode two will also have the welcome bon fire and beach barbecue—including free-flowing drinks. The twist is that the cast isn't allowed to eat until all sixteen pass the sugar cookie, sit-up, push-up test." Shelly shot Jonas a hate filled glare for his idea.

Joanne's eyes lit. "I love it."

Shelly breathed in with relief that at least Joanne was happy, even though she was not.

She continued. "At the beach party the host will finally tell the contestants the rules, which are that the SEALs are to be coaches only and it's their female teammates who will be competing against each other."

"So it's the civilians' performances that determines victory or defeat. Wonderful." Joanne smiled.

"We'll also reveal the first challenge that night. That'll

be the protocol for the remainder of the season. The challenges are revealed one at a time. The cast will be in the dark about what's coming in the weeks ahead, to keep them off kilter. And so they can't prepare in advance."

"Good." Joanne nodded again.

"Oh, and although we'll provide coolers full of groceries, after the first night, the teams will be responsible for cooking for themselves over an open fire during their time on the island. There will also be no facilities provided so they'll be bathing in the ocean and taking care of personal matters in the um, bushes."

Joanne nodded again, looking as if she approved.

Meanwhile Shelly tried not to think about what the future held for her, thanks to Jonas's brilliant idea that they should make it as hard as possible on the cast. And Lucy's whole-hearted agreement that people not used to 'roughing it' made for good television.

It was a sick business she'd chosen as a career. The three of them had come up with more and more crazy ideas as the night stretched on and they became more delirious, all to torture the cast, of which she was one.

And Joanne loved every idea. Stifling a sigh, Shelly continued.

"Episode three starts with the eight teams training for the first challenge and ends with the actual challenge—a four-mile run in boots while carrying a full pack. The slowest contestant will mean that team is out."

"You'll be announcing which team is being disqualified at the start of the following episode to build suspense," Joanne said in what sounded like more of a statement of fact than a question.

"Of course." Shelly nodded, pretending that had been their plan all along.

She saw Jonas scribbling the change into his notes as she cleared her throat and hit a key on the laptop to change to the next slide.

"Episode four will open with the disqualification of the losing team of challenge number one," she ad-libbed. "Then it will feature the remaining seven teams training for challenge number two—the one-mile ocean swim while wearing swim fins."

No one seemed to care at last night's meeting that she'd never worn swim fins before. Or swam a mile in open water before. Or that they hadn't confirmed with all of the female cast that they could actually swim at all, never mind in the ocean, and not drown.

They were going to need lifeguards, a medical team and a hefty insurance policy for this show. She ignored the challenges, put on a happy face, and switched to the next slide.

"Episode five will feature the remaining six teams in challenge number three, land navigation. The competitors will train with their SEAL coaches. The last to find their way back to basecamp will be disqualified. That will be the final challenge on San Clemente Island before we bring the remaining five teams back to Coronado."

Was she only halfway through this presentation? The stress was going to kill her.

Hot Seal, Under Pressure

She dared to glance at Joanne. A look of approval from the executive producer had Shelly feeling a bit better as she advanced to the next slide.

"Episode six will have the five teams training for challenge number four—fast roping. Usually done from a helicopter, we've gotten permission to do ours from the tower on the obstacle course on base. Episode seven features challenge number five for the four remaining teams—sharp shooting. If we can't get approval to use the range on base, we'll just go to a public shooting range."

She paused, got no objection from Joanne, then reached for the computer. "Episode eight features challenge number six with the four remaining teams participating—parachuting." Just saying the word —*parachuting*—had Shelly's heart thundering.

Joanne shaking her head stopped Shelly from moving on. "Wait. I need to confer with legal about this one. Hang on."

Joanne stood and Shelly's hope grew. Joanne could cancel the parachute challenge with one word. And Shelly would be thrilled if she did.

Heights were not her thing. Like not at all. She might just pass out if they made her jump out of a plane. And then she wouldn't be able to pull the rip cord and she'd die.

The worst part was that her death on film would skyrocket ratings, so Joanne might not even care.

She'd told Lucy and Jonas her fear last night.

They didn't seem to believe her. Or maybe they just

thought her paralyzing fear would make for a good episode. She didn't know. But if Joanne came back and said it was a no go, she might have to do a happy dance right up there in front of the PowerPoint presentation.

If Joanne nixed this idea, they would have to come up with another challenge. Lucy and Jonas looked concerned. Meanwhile, Shelly had to control her glee at the possibility.

Finally, Joanne returned. "Legal agreed it's too dangerous to have amateurs skydiving alone."

Shelly's heart leapt.

"So it has to be tandem jumps."

Her joy fell flat as Joanne continued.

"Tandem jumps?" she asked, fearing she knew what that meant.

"The SEAL and the civilian will be strapped together for the jump."

"Oh." Her and Stefan, strapped together. Great.

It was bad enough she was tied to him as his teammate but for this they'd be literally tied together.

His hard body, strapped to hers...

Shelly wrestled her attention back to the presentation. "Um, where was I?"

"Parachute challenge," Jonas supplied.

"Yeah. So the loser will be determined by which team lands farthest from the marked X on the ground."

"The LZ," Jonas piped in again.

"Yes. The landing zone," Shelly repeated, starting to like her assistant less and less the more *helpful* he became.

"Sounds good." Joanne nodded.

Moving on... She needed to wrap this thing up. She was shaking.

She didn't know if that was from adrenaline and thoughts of all she needed to get done to make this show a reality starting the moment this meeting broke, or fear over all the things she'd signed up to do, most of which she couldn't do and had no hope of doing.

Either way, her hand shook as she clicked to the next slide.

She took a deep breath and continued.

"Episode nine will feature challenge number seven, which is the culmination of the season, the timed obstacle course. The final two teams, head-to-head. It'll focus on training on the course. The finalists can request that any of the previously disqualified teams return to help them train with the winner of the prior challenge getting first pick. The episode will end with the actual competition—the running of the course."

"I love it. You'll make sure two of the SEAL coaches coming back are Zach and Nick if they've been eliminated before then."

So much for keeping the *real* in reality.

"Of course," Shelly agreed with Joanne even though manipulating the contestants rubbed her the wrong way.

"And finally, episode ten is a celebration. All of the teams will return for a wrap party and a viewing of the highlights and bloopers from the season. And, the most important part, at the very end we announce the winner of the final challenge and the cash prize."

"Excellent. Great job." Joanne's slow clap might be the biggest compliment the woman had ever given. Shelly was reveling in it when Joanne added, "One thing. Who do we have hosting?"

The question was like nails on a chalkboard. A needle scratching across a vinyl record. Unpleasant. Unexpected. And the one Shelly was unprepared for. The question she had no answer for.

They'd been too busy ironing out the challenges to even think about a list of possible hosts.

"We, uh, hadn't settled on that yet. Do you have a suggestion?" she asked.

"Clay and Tasha," Joanne declared with certainty.

Shelly opened her mouth to protest when Joanne held up one hand, palm forward, to silence her.

"I know Clay said they wouldn't compete with her pregnant. But he didn't say they wouldn't host."

That was technically true, although knowing Clay, Shelly didn't think he cared about technicalities.

"Okay. I'll ask," she agreed since she was sure Joanne would be happy with nothing less.

Joanne had already stood but before she moved toward the door, she said, "Oh, and Shelly. Talk to *her* alone without Clay there. I think you'll get a very different answer from Tasha."

It was sneaky, but Shelly couldn't deny, Joanne was right.

13

San Clemente Island. Stefan had been there before. He'd never forget the place.

Part of California's Channel Islands, San Clemente was owned by the US Navy and administered by Naval Base Coronado, so it was used for tactical training and testing.

Stefan wouldn't say he had good memories of his time here on 'the rock', but he'd never forget the torturous time he spent here during BUD/S.

And now, surreally, he was back here again for this bull shit show for a different kind of torture. The kind that came with twenty-four/seven cameras up his ass. And a cute but clueless teammate.

He stared at Shelly now as she dragged her gear off to the brush.

"What are you doing?" he asked.

"Picking a spot to camp," she huffed.

"In the brush?"

"Yes. It's out of the way. So it'll be more quiet and private."

"Yup. Just the kind of conditions wildlife prefers when it slithers or creeps into some tourist's tent," he commented.

She stopped dead and she dumped everything she held onto the ground.

"Where should I set up?" she asked, the frustration clear in her tone.

That wasn't encouraging. They'd arrived five minutes ago and she was already unhappy.

Biting his tongue when he really wanted to tell her and everyone else there what he thought of this game they'd set up, he pointed to the open area of sand where he'd dropped the gear he'd been assigned by the crew. "Right here. Next to mine."

"Fine," she huffed and dragged her stuff toward his.

She had nothing to complain about. He was there, wasn't he? And she probably didn't realize it, but she was damn lucky he was keeping his language mostly clean for the cameras.

Hell, he'd even sat down and talked about himself while staring into a camera lens like an idiot when she'd sent a crew to his barracks last night for her stupid introduction episode.

This was him being nice. She should probably be more appreciative and less annoyed. Although she was likely more annoyed with the gear than with him.

Speaking of the gear...

"Do we know what they packed for us?" he asked, eying what looked like a tent, a sleeping bag and not much more.

"Nope."

He glanced up at her. "I thought you planned this."

"I did. The episodes and the challenges. And I saw the website and the social media plan. But this—" She swept a gaze around them. It looked like a sporting goods store had exploded. "This is a different department."

"Great." He bent to unzip a bag he'd carried that had made an intriguing clanging sound as he'd dropped it.

Time to see what they were in for.

He pulled out a camp stove, a pot, a tin plate and cup and a spoon and glanced up at her. "We have to cook?"

She nodded. "Every meal while we're here except for tonight's."

"You know, there's a perfectly good chow hall here that they use during trainings. Beds and toilets and showers too." He hooked a thumb toward the other part of the island as he realized the one thing he hadn't spotted in the bag was a roll of toilet paper.

"Survivor," she huffed out while dragging her folded tent open.

"Survivor?" he repeated, confused.

She straightened and pushed a stray piece of hair out of her eyes.

Her cheeks were pink from the excursion as she said, "Twenty-two years and forty-two seasons and *Survivor* is still going strong. Viewers like to watch other people roughing it while they sit in the comfort of their own homes."

"So we have to cook over a fire and shit in the sand with leaves for toilet paper to make the viewing public happy?"

"Exactly." She nodded before bending to pick up a tent pole. She alternated staring at it and the tent on the ground before looking up at him. "Do you know how to do this?"

"Yes," he answered.

"Will you help me?" She widened her eyes expectantly.

Seeing an opportunity, he grinned. "Depends. What will you give me in exchange?"

Her frown was fast and furious. "I'm not sleeping with you for it, that's for damn sure."

He bit out a few choice words that the network censors wouldn't approve of before returning her frown. "Believe me. Sex with you here is the dead last thing on my mind. That wasn't what I was talking about at all, so get your mind out of the gutter."

"Then what were you talking about?" she demanded.

She crossed her arms, which made her tits strain the fabric of her T-shirt and made a liar out of him since he was definitely thinking about sex with her, here, now.

He cleared his mind of that thought and said, "I want information."

"What kind of information?" she asked.

"Whatever you can give me about the other teams or anything about the challenges that will help me—us—win."

He'd have to split the money with her, but half was better than none. And the glory of the win would be all his.

She frowned again and he began to suspect he'd be seeing that expression from her a lot this week. "I can't do that. It wouldn't be ethical."

"And your boss forcing me to participate in this shit show or risk my military career is?"

She pressed her lips together. "I am sorry about that. I had nothing to do with it."

He believed her.

"I can tell you this," she continued and he leaned in closer to hear. "The cameras are on twenty-four hours a day and they have night vision so don't think darkness is any protection. The sound team is on site so expect anything you say can and will be recorded. The mics are amazing and catch everything, even long range. So no more talk *about cheating*." She mouthed the last two words silently so he had to read her lips.

"*Okay*," he mouthed back, just as silently.

Then he let out another single silent word over the information she'd shared. Cameras. Mics. Night vision. *Fuck.*

"So when will we be told what's happening?" he asked as a scowl settled on his face. He didn't like being kept in the dark.

"As soon as we get these tents set up, we're to meet on the beach for a barbecue. Then they'll explain the first challenge and the rules of the game to us."

"As soon as these tents are up? Then I can find out what the hell is going on *and* I get fed?" he asked, just to clarify.

"Yup." She nodded. "And there's alcohol too."

His brows rose. "Step aside, sweetie. I got this."

Lucky for him, all the SEALs had realized the same thing he had. The quicker they did the work for their female civilian teammates, the sooner they could get this show on the road—so to speak.

In no time they were assembled along the surf where Stefan kept reminding himself he was no longer a trainee and was not here to be tortured by instructors. Still, the whole island made him twitch.

Where was that alcohol Shelly had promised him?

He glanced around looking for a cooler he could pilfer when the action around him picked up and the conversation died down.

A camera followed the dark-haired man he'd seen talking to Shelly that first day by the O-course. Clay, was it? This time, the guy was with a hot chick.

"Who's this now?" he whispered.

"That's Clay and his fiancé Tasha, from *Hot House*. They agreed to host our show."

Host. What did that even mean? Stefan guessed he'd soon figure out what a host did as lights flipped on and the camera closed in on the two.

"Welcome to San Clemente Island. I'm Tasha," she said with a smile as she looked to her male counterpart.

"I'm Clay," the guy grumbled.

"And we're your hosts for *Under Pressure*, the show that asks the question, could you be a Navy SEAL? During the following weeks these eight civilians will find out, as they are put to the test, performing many of the tasks their SEAL teammates had to master to earn that coveted Navy SEAL trident. We'll explain more about the competition and the challenges later. But first, Clay." Tasha turned the focus over to Clay.

"During BUD/S, as trainees we don't get to rest or eat without working for it first. The same goes for here," Clay said looking a bit too cocky that he wasn't one of the participants, just the host delivering the bad news. "Since there's no challenge today, the workout to earn your place at tonight's barbecue is sugar cookies, followed by twenty-push-ups in the sand."

"SEALs, take your civilians down to the surf and demonstrate the proper sugar cookie technique. No one eats until all of you are sugared and have counted off twenty push-ups," Tasha yelled.

She'd had to raise her voice to be heard over the grumbling of the SEALs and the whispered questions of some of the civilians who had no clue what sugar cookies were.

But there was one civilian who definitely knew what they were. The person who was in charge of planning these stunts.

Stefan shot Shelly a glare. "Sugar cookies. Really? So now we have to sit in wet sandy clothes to eat?"

"That was Jonas's idea. Not mine. I didn't even know what sugar cookies were except for, you know, a cookie, until he told me. The damn kid's brother must be a SEAL or something because he knows way too much about all the shit that comes with your training. More than a normal assistant should."

She drew in a breath then struggled to her feet from the log on which they'd been sitting. The producers of this show didn't even provide folding chairs.

Shelly glanced down at him once she was on her feet. "Come on. Let's get this over with. With any luck, they packed us a change of clothes for after."

"They better have," he grumbled as he followed her toward the water's edge.

He'd already done his share of sugar cookies in his lifetime. And now he was doing more. And he was going to be cold and sandy all night, *plus* he'd have to listen to Shelly complain about being cold and sandy on top of his own discomfort.

Dragging his feet to delay the inevitable, he was still yards behind her when she ran into the surf, fully clothed, dipped down to her neck, then stood and turned to face him.

He tripped over his own bare feet when he got an eyeful of the vision she made coming out of the water. It could have been a scene from a James Bond movie where all the women were insanely attractive and, for some reason, so often dripping wet.

This—her—and his notice of her was one thing he hadn't anticipated. Although he should have, given the fact Shelly was wearing a white shirt that was now soaked in sea water. A thin cotton T-shirt that clung to her curves like a second skin after her plunge into the cold water.

Not even the coating of sand after she'd dropped to the shore and rolled could cover the hard peaks of her nipples. Nor did it detract from the vision this woman made.

He swallowed hard as she then dropped to her knees on the sand to start her push-ups.

"Are you counting?" she gasped after her second push-up.

Shelly. On her knees. Right there in front of him. Hell, no he hadn't been counting.

She raised her head to glance up at him when he didn't answer.

He remained dry, upright and was currently speechless from staring down at the wet cotton shorts molded to her ass.

"Uh, yeah. Two," he announced, pretending he'd been right on top of things this whole time.

She did her twenty reps like a trooper. Meanwhile, he had yet to move from where his feet were planted in the sand.

There was one positive to this whole situation, though.

Running into that frigid water was going to be a welcome deterrent to the growing situation inside his shorts.

There should be points awarded in this game for resisting your hot-as-hell teammate. If there were, he'd win that competition too.

As he glanced around, he noticed there was more than one SEAL who had the same dazed expression he no doubt wore. More than one set of eyes trying to avoid looking where they shouldn't, while a couple of others blatantly stared and enjoyed the show.

And in the background, as the crew watched eagerly from behind the scenes, occasionally pointing and whispering, he realized this was exactly what the network wanted.

Survivor? Bull shit. It wasn't the survival aspect of this show they were counting on to get ratings.

They—the production company and more importantly the viewing public—wanted sex. And this show was designed to give it to them, right down to the mixed sex teams and this little impromptu wet T-shirt contest.

And thanks to command, he was smack in the middle of it. Mother fuc—

"Your turn," Shelly announced, brushing her palms together to knock the sand from them.

"Uh, yup," he agreed, his voice sounding husky to his ears.

He plunged into the icy water and barely even felt it.

14

Somebody was going to get a talking to.

Shelly made that vow as she sat, miserable and cold, covered in sand and tried not to scowl as the cameraman pulled in for a tight shot on her and Stefan, who sat equally sandy on the log next to her.

There were no extra clothes packed for them to change into. The bastards.

She couldn't even take solace in the fact that Gabby and Dani, as well as Nick and Zach, looked equally miserable because they also looked pissed off about the whole thing, and she couldn't blame them.

However, they were most likely blaming her for their current unpleasant situation. As Stefan kept reminding her, this was her show idea and she'd planned the episodes.

How had things spiraled out of her control? Her fun competition had turned into torture. Between Jonas and his good ideas and Joanne with her lust for ratings, Shelly should be grateful they weren't catching their own fish for food or eating maggots for the challenges.

"Now for the reading of the rules and the reveal of the first challenge," Tasha said, looking beautiful. And dry. And not covered in sand. She turned to her soon-to-be husband. "Clay?"

Clay nodded. "Competitors are only as good as the coaches behind them—"

"That's not true," Stefan mumbled.

Shelly shushed him as Clay continued. "So for the duration of the competition, the SEALs will not compete and will act as coaches only. Their job is to prepare their civilian teammates.

Tasha took over in the tag team hosting. "The women will represent their team and compete against each other for the upcoming challenges."

Clay jumped back in saying, "SEALs, remember, your teammate's win is your win. Their loss, is your loss."

"The first challenge tomorrow will be the four-mile run," Tasha announced.

"In boots and a full pack," Clay added. That was followed by a chorus of groans, which only made him break into an uncharacteristic smile.

"What?" Stefan spun to glare at her. "I don't get to compete? Only you? How did that happen?

"Jonas," Shelly said simply. She realized it was becoming her answer for a lot of things.

Stefan shook his head. "This Jonas person better not

come anywhere near me or I can't promise what I'll do to him."

"Noted." She nodded.

"Four-miles." Stefan sighed. "Are you at least a runner?"

"Yes. I run every day," she answered with satisfaction.

"Okay. Good. How far?" he asked, perking up a bit.

"I do an hour on the treadmill every morning before work while I check my email on my iPad." Ha! That would teach him to be a doubter.

He visibly wilted. "Not the same. Not the same at all. And you're definitely not running in boots, long pants and a full pack while you're *checking your email* on the treadmill."

"Well, yeah. You got me there. I only break out my boots and pack for special occasions." She scowled.

He ignored her snark as he appeared lost in thought. "We just have to hope the rest of these Barbie dolls are into doing yoga and getting smoothies at the gym and that they're slower than you. That's the only chance we have to win tomorrow."

"Win?" She blew out a lip-flapping breath. "You do know if we lose you can go home and this whole nightmare will be over."

His eyes flew wide in horror. "If we lose, we don't win any money. And my team will mock me forever."

"Why? *I'll* be the one who lost. Not you."

He scowled. "No. We're a team. You heard them. Your loss is my loss."

"Great. Thanks. No pressure there." She rolled her eyes. "And you know, every single thing they said up there was scripted by some lackey back at the office in San Diego. Don't take it as gospel just because it came out of Clay's mouth. It's not some SEAL credo."

"I know that. And just so *you* know, the actual SEAL credo, as you call it, which I don't need Clay to tell me, is *the only easy day was yesterday*."

"Well, it might have been yesterday but it's sure *not* going to be tomorrow." She stood and brushed what drying sand she could off her clothes. "I'm going to bed."

"Good idea." He pouted.

Thank God they at least had separate tents. She escaped into hers where she could do some pouting of her own in private.

15

The next morning came too soon. The sun rose fast on an island.

Shelly was used to rising early so she was already attempting to make a fire by rubbing two sticks together when Stefan appeared. But he didn't come from out of his tent, as she expected. He came jogging up the beach with a bag.

She leaned back on her heels and watched him approach, not worrying she'd lose any progress with the fire building by taking a break since she hadn't made any progress except for making her arms tired.

"Are you so jealous of me doing the run today alone you decided to do your own?" she asked.

"Maybe." He glanced around them before squatting down beside her. Making eye contact, he pressed one finger to his lips to silence her, then opened the bag he carried.

Her eyes widened as he pulled out a box of matches. "Where?"

He shushed her, then glanced around again before leaning close.

"I know from when I was here during BUD/S that the chow hall is never locked. I grabbed what I could," he whispered against her ear.

She felt the warmth of his breath brush against her skin. It sent a shiver through her that had nothing to do with the crisp morning air.

But more than the fact her insides were feeling a bit squishy thanks to Stefan's intimate whisper, what he said had her eyes flying wider.

He'd snuck off and robbed a military facility she hadn't even been aware was on this island? She too glanced around to make sure no cameras where in sight.

"There's also a phone in there," he continued. "I called a buddy. He's dropping off clothes for us. We'll get caught if we wear them out here in front of the cameras, but we can at least have on dry underwear and something not sandy to sleep in inside the tents."

Her mouth fell open as a dozen questions swirled in her mind at his revelations though not one of them mattered.

What was done, was done. And if they did get caught, Joanne would eat it up. Navy SEALs could do no wrong in her eyes. She'd love him showing initiative by sneaking off and robbing the chow hall.

Stefan had tossed a few more sticks and some dry

leaves into her fire pit and after one more visual sweep of the area, dropped a lit match into the pile. The fire sprang to life, which it never would have if she'd still been rubbing two sticks together.

As he opened his bag again, she spotted packages of instant coffee and also instant oatmeal.

"The show is providing food, you know," she told him, not that she didn't appreciate his efforts. Especially the roll of toilet paper she'd also seen inside the bag.

"Before I left for my '*run*', I saw one of the team guys gutting a fish while his assigned Model Barbie turned green like she was about to puke. Fish—head, scales, tail and all. *That's* what they're providing for us to cook for breakfast. They're taking the *Survivor* aspect a little too far, if you ask me."

Fish for breakfast? She had been thinking more like eggs, bacon and coffee when she made this plan.

She cringed. "I guess I should have specified the menu items in my proposal."

"I'd agree except that I'm not sure those in charge would have taken your suggestions. It seems they're determined to torture us."

She had to agree with him. "I'm sorry."

He shook his head. "Not your fault. Don't worry. I've been tortured by better than these people. And on this very island, as a matter of fact. I've got a few tricks of my own up my sleeves."

A strange feeling of camaraderie mixed with gratitude

gave her a full, warm feeling inside. She was finding it hard to be annoyed with him today.

"Thank—" she began, but stopped when he lifted his head, like a dog on a hunt. "What? Did you hear something? Was it a snake?"

Her gaze flew to the ground as she tried to look everywhere at once.

She'd slept horribly last night wondering what animals were creeping around outside her tent.

San Clemente was used for Navy trainings, but this part where the production team had chosen to set up their camp was particularly desolate. It felt as if they were on a completely uninhabited island.

A raven cawed loudly overhead, startling her. She ducked lower and covered her head with both hands.

He frowned at her reaction. "No. I heard a…" He looked around them, his head on a swivel like a bobblehead on a dashboard. "*Zodiac*."

Now it was her turn to frown at his final hissed word.

"What's a zodiac?" she replied in an exaggerated stage-whisper.

He rolled his eyes. "Come with me and *be quiet*."

Stefan grabbed her with one big rough hand and tugged—practically dragged—her through the bushes toward the beach.

"And for your information, if you ever do *hear* a snake when you're back on the mainland, it's probably a rattler. So freeze, locate where it is, then back away *slowly* or you're dead."

"Ha-ha," she said flatly as he obviously tried to frighten her.

He glanced at her, brows high. "I'm not kidding."

Holy shit.

She glanced back behind them, half in hopes someone was following them so she had an excuse to go back to the fire and not further into the brush, which looked like a pretty good place to her for a snake to live.

No wonder Dani had quit her job at NMM after *Cold Feet* wrapped. This on-location shit was insane.

She tripped, but Stefan kept her from going down when her foot caught on a rock—which had only happened because he was dragging her along much too fast for this rough terrain. She was out of breath and patience when she saw it. An inflatable boat with the five SEALs she'd met on the obstacle course inside.

"Did they take that all the way here from San Diego?" she asked.

He frowned at her. "No. That would take too long. There's a ferry. Although knowing these guys, they probably talked their way onto one of the flights headed here. Then grabbed the Zodiac from the training facility to get to us. SEALs can be very inventive when they need to be."

"I'm starting to realize that."

Like they were storming the beach for an attack, they leapt over the sides into the shallow water, each grabbing the boat and pulling it up onto the beach.

It was a beautiful thing, the precision with which they operated. Separate but one in motion and purpose.

The producer inside Shelly wanted to catch the action on tape.

The human in her was easily sidetracked from that thought when one—the SEAL she recognized as Mason—leaned over, reached inside the boat and emerged with a Starbucks bag.

She nearly fell to her knees at the sight and the anticipation.

Next to her, Stefan looked less excited as he planted his feet wide and folded his arms. "I didn't expect this to be a team operation."

"If you think you can call one of us for something like this and not get all of us then you've lost your damn mind." The guy whose name she remembered was Danny laughed.

Sniffing, Stefan shook his head. "You guys must be really bored."

"This is the most fun we've had since getting back from—" Mason didn't finish the sentence as his gaze shot to her.

Flirt grabbed the bag from Mason's hand and moved forward to stand in front of her. "Good morning. Coffee?"

"God, yes," she answered with breathy enthusiasm.

"That's what she said." The mumbled comment from one of the SEALs was followed by chuckles from a few of the others and Shelly didn't care.

Her icy hand was wrapped around a hot cup of coffee.

Then that coffee was careening down her throat, warming her from the inside, fueling her spirit and her body.

Her eyes flitted closed as she let out an open-mouthed breath.

"Jeez, I need to start bringing women coffee instead of flowers if this is the reaction." Flirt laughed.

She opened her eyes and saw Flirt's dimples on full display as he smiled and watched her drink. "Being a castaway on a deserted island tends to make you appreciate the little things."

"*Little* is what I heard when it comes to Flirt." The joke came from another undisclosed SEAL she couldn't see behind the wall of muscle as Flirt blocked her view.

He shook his head. "Don't listen to them."

"Never even considered it." She was too busy having a love affair with her Starbucks *Venti*.

He'd even added cream and sugar, just the way she liked it. How was that?

"How did you know how I take my coffee?" she asked.

He smiled, his green eyes twinkling with mischief as he lifted one shoulder. "Lucky guess."

"Dickhead." Stefan was next to her, scowling at Flirt before he turned to face her. "I told him how you take it."

Stefan had another bag in his hand. This one with a familiar chain store logo on it. He thrust it at her. "Here. It's not much but it's dry and warm... I guessed at your sizes."

She juggled the coffee, which she refused to set down,

and the bag that she held in her free hand. She finally maneuvered and got a peek inside.

There she saw what looked like new underwear, socks, a sweatshirt and sweatpants.

She glanced up at Stefan. "You bought me underwear?"

"Hey. We both could have used some dry underwear last night after those damn sugar cookies we did," Stefan bit out, sounding defensive.

"Sugar cookies?" Danny let out a hearty laugh. "Excellent. I hope that's on video for us to see. No wonder you needed new skivvies."

The man she remembered as Eric from the release forms snorted. "I can tell you, that was a fun shopping trip to the ladies' lingerie aisle."

"Yeah. Heads up. We might be banned from that store now," Wyatt warned.

"You shouldn't have fought with me about what to buy," Flirt accused Wyatt.

"Who knew it would be such a contentious decision between boy shorts and bikinis." Danny shook his head.

"Don't forget the thongs." Flirt grinned.

Stefan blew out a curse and shot Flirt a glare. "Shut up, man."

Shelly let out a breathy laugh.

Being angry at any of these guys—even with their juvenile jokes—seemed out of the question. She was too grateful for the small comforts they'd delivered. She turned to Stefan, who was still scowling at Flirt.

"Thank you for this." She held up the coffee and the bag. "For all of it."

His attention moved from his teammate to her. Their eyes met and held. For the first time she noticed the color of his. Hazel with flecks of gold and a tinge of green that drew and held her attention.

For a moment he didn't say a word. The silence lasted so long she wondered if something was wrong. Finally, he tipped his head in a nod.

"You're welcome." He cleared his throat and took the Starbucks bag from Flirt, glancing to see what else was inside. "We gotta eat and drink up so we can get back before anyone misses us."

"There's food too?" she asked, almost afraid to wish for it.

"Of course. Your wish is my command, my lady." Flirt delivered a courtly bow to her.

Stefan grumbled something, but she didn't hear it because he'd just unwrapped and held out a bacon, egg and cheese sandwich to her.

Next to the promise of that in her mouth—and in her belly—

nothing else mattered in the world.

16

"What's your advice? You're the coach. How do I run for four miles while carrying *that*? Help me." The frustration in Shelly's voice translated clearly.

Stefan glanced up from the pack the crew had given her for the run. "I am helping you."

"It doesn't look like it. It looks like you're pilfering the supplies."

"Is that what you think I'm doing? Yeah, sure. Because I'm going to have a lot of use for all this ammo with no gun." He rolled his eyes and began to reach for what he'd unloaded from the pack and laid out on the tent's floor.

She let out a huff, standing just outside the tent's opening with her hand planted on one hip. They had her in combat boots and shorts for this challenge. Not exactly regulation, but he wasn't surprised the producers wanted to show off the females' legs.

Ratings. A word he hoped to never hear again once he walked away from this show—hopefully with wads of cash in his pocket.

He pulled his eyes away from Shelly's long, tempting limbs and up to her pouty lips, although not before noticing how the crisp white T-shirt they'd given her with the cargo shorts accentuated her tits nicely.

"I'm repacking this for you. To redistribute the weight. It'll be easier if the heavier stuff is near the top. Novices make the mistake of putting the heavy stuff at the bottom. Doing that will fuck you up after the first mile."

"Oh. Okay. Thank you."

He glanced at her feet. "Sit down and retie those boots."

"Why?" she asked.

"You want them tight all the way up to the top to provide support for your ankles. It's rough terrain. You're going to step wrong out there. You don't want a twisted ankle."

She must have accepted his reasoning since she dropped down onto the sand and started to untie one boot.

"You have your new underwear on?" he asked.

Her eyes flew up before she narrowed them to glare at him.

"I'm not being a perv. You need good socks and underwear for a run like this or you're going to chafe."

"I have on the new socks and yes, the underwear."

"Good. Now during the run," he began as he zipped

up one filled compartment and moved on to packing the next. "Don't start out at a run."

"I thought running is the point."

"No. Not finishing last is the point. And if you start out too fast, you'll exhaust yourself. And a full out run is just going to make the pack keep whacking you in the back with every step."

He'd asked her to clarify the rules and she'd actually agreed and told him. They didn't have to win the challenges to make it to the end of this competition. Just not be eliminated. The final challenge was where the money was awarded.

They only had to not come in last in the run today. And with Shelly as the one competing, not coming in last was the best he was willing to hope for.

He hated it but it was true. He had to put his own need to be first in all things aside for this.

It was hard, but he'd do it.

"Let the others take off fast and tire themselves out," he continued. "You pace yourself. Keep an eye on where the others are. Stay in the middle of the pack. Just cross that finish line before one other person and we're golden."

"Okay." She was agreeing with him but not looking as if she believed what he said.

At least not deep inside where it mattered. In that place where motivation lived. Where you drew from when things got rough and you wanted to give up.

He finished repacking the bag and carried it out to

where she sat on the sand looking exhausted before the run had even started.

"Listen to me. I've had to march in full kit for far longer than four miles."

Her scowl told him he'd started badly.

"The point is, you can do it, even when you think you can't. You can. You have to believe that."

She looked visibly defeated. He reached out and took her hands. "Your feet will be on the trail. But your head can be wherever you want to be. What's your dream spot?"

"My sofa in front of the television."

God help them.

He drew in a breath. "All right. We'll work with that. During the run, you want to think of anything else but the weight on your back. Imagine yourself there on your sofa in front of the TV. What are you watching? What are you wearing? What snacks are you munching on? The first quarter mile is the hardest. Once you get through that, it all becomes a blur of sameness so let your mind go to your happy place."

She nodded. "Okay. I can do that."

He delivered what he hoped was an encouraging smile. "Good. You'll be fine. And when you get back, I'll be waiting to fix up all of your blisters."

"Blisters," she repeated, wide-eyed.

Shit. He needed to stop talking now.

17

"You did great, Shell. Really good."

Shelly heard Stefan, but couldn't see him against the glare of the sun above where she lay flat on her back on the ground at base camp.

"Please make sure no snakes get me. I don't think I can move."

"There are no snakes here on this island. Although the wild goats will get pretty close and try to steal your food."

She managed to open her eyes. "Why didn't you tell me that before?"

"About the goats?"

"Not the goats. The snakes. I've been a wreck worrying about snakes."

He lifted one shoulder. "Sorry. And you can move if you just try. Sit up. Drink some water."

She tried to lift her arm to take the bottle he extended

to her, but the limb fell back to the ground. "Nope. Can't do it."

"Yes, you can. Come on. I'll help you."

She felt him yanking her arm but didn't feel compelled to help in any way. Finally, he got her into a sitting position, propped up against his body as he tried handing her the bottle again.

This time she managed to take it. "How can my whole body be sweating but I'm cold. And the top of my head is tingling."

He mumbled something that sounded like cuss words before he said, "Drink more of that water. Then you need to change into dry clothes."

She managed another sip before she said, "Are my feet bleeding? They feel like they're bleeding. Except for the parts that are numb."

More cuss words followed. "We'll get your boots off in a bit. Rest now."

"What place did I come in?" she asked when her brain started to function again and death wasn't uppermost in her mind.

"Fourth."

"Hey. Look at that. You told me to stay in the middle of the pack and I finished right in the middle. That's pretty good. Right?" It was getting easier to breathe and talk. But she'd give anything for a nice shower. Or maybe a bath. A shower would require being upright and on her painful feet.

"Very good," he agreed, as she began to think he was just humoring her.

He was being too nice. It was strange. Maybe she was delirious.

A thought hit her. "Who won?"

"Stone faced Barbie." Stefan's answer vibrated through her.

She realized she was still using him as a prop and decided it was time she sat up. She managed to do that and turned to glance at him. "Who?"

"The one who has that serious pissed off look on her face all the time," he elaborated. "Like those pinched faced models on runways in Milan."

She would have laughed at how accurate his description was if it would have required more air than she was willing to demand from her exhausted lungs. "She won?"

"Yup. Turned out to be a ringer. She's some sort of marathon runner."

"Hmm." She couldn't muster more of a reaction than that.

"You hungry?"

"I think so. But I also think I might puke if I try to eat now. I'll wait until after the elimination ceremony. I probably should get myself cleaned up for that."

No. Fuck it. She was beyond caring how she looked on camera at this point.

"The what ceremony?" he asked.

"Elimination. Tasha and Clay are coming back to reveal who came in last."

"Why? We know who came in last. I was there. I saw it. We all did."

"You saw it, but the viewers won't. They'll edit the episode so you can't tell who came in last at the end. So the viewers will have to wait until the beginning of the next episode to find out who lost. Who was it anyway? The last one in." She couldn't believe she'd forgotten to ask until now.

"Airhead Barbie," he answered moving around to start to unlace her boots.

She let him as she reviewed the cast and couldn't place who he meant. "Who?"

Where was he getting these names from? And should she be writing them down for the producers to use?

"The one who asks all the dumb questions all the time."

"Oh, her. Okay, good."

"Why good?" he asked. "Besides the fact the Q&A will be cut in at least half without her."

"Because I'd hate to lose Flirty Barbie or Backstabbing Barbie this early in the show. They're good for ratings."

He chuckled. "I know exactly which two you're talking about."

She hated to admit it and felt like a traitor to her sex, but she couldn't deny that the Barbie naming system was working for them.

"Ready?" he asked, holding her loosened boot in one hand and her calf in the other.

"Go ahead. But if there's blood, I don't want to see."

He tugged off the boot and with it came a searing pain.

She felt him roll off her sock. "Oh yeah. That's a nice blister. It popped too."

"Great."

"A little soak in the salt water and you'll feel better." He pulled the second boot and sock off.

She hissed at the pain then attempted to wiggle her numb toes. "Can't wait."

"Hey, at least you don't have to put those boots right back on like I had to," he said.

"But I'm not in BUD/S training like you were, so..."

She should be sitting at her desk in the nice air-conditioned office. Not freezing in the surf or sweating during a four-mile run.

"And I'm only here because of you, so..." He bobbed his head to the side.

She sighed. He was right. It was her own fault that she was there too. She needed to keep her ideas to herself.

"Will there be alcohol at this elimination ceremony?" he asked as he stood.

"God. I hope so." She struggled to stand and failed. He extended a hand to help her up. "They'll announce the names of the team leaving and very dramatically tell them to pack their tents and leave the island. We'll all hug them and pretend to be sad. Then we're done for the night."

"Done. Pfft. Not quite. We still have to make a fire and cook dinner."

As he said that, a four-wheeler drove up with Clay and Tasha inside.

Stefan glared. "Are they staying in the barracks building here?"

"I don't know. Maybe. Or they're bringing them over when we need them." At his deep scowl, she poked him with her elbow. "Cheer up. Envy isn't a good look on you."

His frown deepened. "Next show I wanna be the host."

"You'd do another show?" she asked, genuinely surprised.

His gaze shot to her. "No. It's just an expression."

"Well don't say it in front of Joanne."

"Why not?"

She blew out a laugh. "Talk to Zach about what happened to him. Or to Clay. Or to Nick. Joanne has a way of sucking you in and making you do things you don't want to."

"Like sucking you into being a contestant?" he asked.

Shelly nodded. "And like *you* into being a contestant. I wanted Flirt for the cast. Joanne chose you instead."

He drew back and shot her a comically unhappy glare. "Flirt? Why? Because he's *so cute*."

She laughed at his unflattering voice.

"Yes." She decided to cut him a break and added,

"And because he, unlike you, had actually signed his release form without duress."

He pulled his mouth to the side. "Mmm. Do me a favor?"

"What?"

"Never ever tell Flirt you wanted him for the show. He'll be impossible to live with otherwise."

"Will you build the fire and do the cooking tonight if I do?" she asked.

"Since I'd like to eat before midnight and I saw your fire-starting skills at breakfast, yes, I will."

"All right. My silence for your cooking. Deal?"

"Deal," he mumbled on a sigh.

And just like that, a truce formed and a partnership was sealed. Good thing, too. She might need his help.

She took one step and winced, stopping where she stood.

"Can't walk?" he asked.

"Not willingly."

He shook his head. "I got you."

Before she knew it, she ended up over his shoulder as he carried her to where Tasha and Clay and the others had gathered.

He set her down and she stumbled to stand, whether that was because her equilibrium was shot from her head hanging upside down or from being swept off her feet by Stefan, she wasn't sure.

She noticed a few glances in her direction. Particularly

from Flirty Barbie. Meanwhile the camera was right there catching it all.

Ratings, she thought, then sat on the log next to Stefan.

"Today, we say goodbye to one of our teams," Tasha began. "Clay. Who will be leaving the island?"

Clay, for a grump, looked like he was getting into his host duties. Either that or he was just enjoying that Zach and Nick had to suffer through the competition and he did not. Either way, he hammed it up as he put on a somber face and said, "Miguel and Tammy, you came in last in the four-mile run. Please ring out and say your goodbyes."

Stefan let out a snort. "That right there adds insult to injury. You didn't tell me they brought a bell."

"I didn't know."

He glanced sideways at her. "I'm starting to think there's a lot you don't know."

"So am I." And she didn't like it. What else had they changed. What other surprises was she in for?

"Bye-bye," Stefan whispered as the SEAL leaving rang the bell solemnly.

She imagined he was envisioning when it would be their turn to leave and he had to ring that bell.

"The remaining seven teams will move on to the next challenge. A one-mile swim."

"In the ocean," Clay added. "In swim fins."

"The swim challenge is here? On the island?" Stefan's eyes were wide as he stared at her.

"Yes. Why? What's wrong?"

He seemed concerned. Meanwhile, she was just grateful—now that she was facing this challenge—that they'd made the decision during that planning meeting to cut the two-mile swim down to one-mile.

He shook his head. "You should have talked to me first. Or to Clay. Or hell, any of the SEALs. We would have told you not to plan the swim for here."

"Why not?" she asked again.

"The water's too rough. The surf here can literally break bones. Then there's the sharks. Not to mention the kelp beds that make it feel like aliens grabbing your legs while you swim through them."

She rolled her eyes at his obvious exaggeration. "I think I'll be fine. You're just trying to scare me."

He lifted a brow. "No. I'm not. I'm not joking, Shelly. It happened during a BUD/S class. A candidate's leg. Broken. And the water's cold. Not uncomfortably cold, but like hypothermia cold. Once, a trainee died of hypothermia after the five-and-a-half-mile swim. Look it up. It's true."

Her eyes widened. "*You* suggested swimming as one of the challenges."

He snorted. "I didn't know you were going to run off and plan it for here. I figured it would be at Coronado. Like in the surf in front of the hotel where it's safe. Hell, they've even moved the BUD/S required swim off this island and to the shore along Coronado. Only a lunatic would swim here willingly."

"You did it," she reminded him.

"As you keep saying, I had to. For BUD/S. And you are not in BUD/S. And I didn't say I was sane at the time. In fact, during those final weeks of BUD/S when the class was already stretched to their limit and training moved to this God forsaken island, sanity was definitely in short supply."

She shook her head. "It should be fine. None of the other SEALs are complaining."

"Because most of them are so old they've forgotten what it's like." He scowled.

"Nick is younger than you," she pointed out.

"All right. Then go ask him what he thinks about this challenge."

One glance over at the pow wow happening between the two couples and Nick's scowl as he shook his head told her Stefan was right.

She didn't need to walk over and ask. It was clear how Zach and Nick felt about the challenge. Especially when they both stood, stalked over to Clay and a really animated discussion began.

"Okay. The other SEALs are not thrilled about that challenge either," she admitted

"Told you." He sighed. "You know, you could go to your boss and say no."

"I could also lose my job."

He evaluated her closer. "How strong a swimmer are you?"

She lifted one shoulder. "I was on the swim team at our town pool every summer during middle school.

During high school I got a job during the summer and couldn't do practice and meets anymore."

His brows rose. "I guess that's better than nothing. You might not die."

She drew in a breath. "Thanks. Your confidence is overwhelming."

He lifted a shoulder then reached into a cooler she hadn't noticed before and thrust a beer toward her. "Beer?"

"Sure. Why not." She took it and downed a good third of the bottle.

Who knew? Judging by the reaction of the SEALs, this beer might be her last. And if it was her final beer and she died tomorrow, and if it turned out it was Jonas who had planned the swim for this god forsaken island, she was definitely going to haunt him for the rest of his life.

18

Stefan took a swig of the subpar coffee he'd been forced to consume that morning.

The cell phone the guys had left for him had no signal so he couldn't even call his teammates to order in breakfast again this morning.

He'd had to make a fire, boil water and deal with the powdered stuff.

Scowling he took the cell out of his pocket again, hoping for some miracle and a few bars.

Shelly came out of her tent and dove at him, shoving his hand with the cell phone down.

"Where did you get that?" she whispered.

"The guys."

"No phones allowed."

"I know. That's why they had to bring me a burner. Because your crew confiscated all our cells. Why is that again?"

"They like to keep the cast isolated and disoriented. So no contact with the outside world. No clocks or watches either so we're never sure what time it is. In some of the shows, they wake them up at the crack of dawn with blasting music and super bright lights after keeping them up until midnight the night before."

"Jesus."

It sounded more fitting for torture employed by terrorists, not entertainment in the free world.

He shook his head. "Doesn't matter anyway. No signal." He stood and tossed the remainder of the coffee into the sand before tossing his useless cell phone into his tent.

"I guess we should get down to preparing for today. What do we know about the competition?" Stefan asked.

"Um—like what?"

"You hired them. Right? So, what are their swimming skills?" he clarified.

"The SEALs should all be strong swimmers—"

"Not talking about the SEALs. The girls. They're the ones competing. What do you know about them?"

"Well, funny thing. The gorgeous women who applied to be on an undisclosed reality show didn't think to include their swimming ability with their headshots." She shot him a glance filled with attitude to match her snarky reply.

"Well, maybe next time you plan a show based on physical abilities, you should ask," he shot back.

He visually swept the field of competitors. Flirty

Barbie had donned a large orange life vest with the help of her partner who took extra time securing all the straps and buckles around her bodacious body.

It looked like he was giving her a lesson in water safety and the proper use of the life jacket. Either that or he was just enjoying the proximity of her tits.

Whatever the reason for the life vest, it probably wasn't a bad idea. Although Stefan knew it would slow the swimmer down.

Since Shelly said she'd been on a swim team, she should have a decent stroke. And she'd be far faster cutting through the water without a life jacket.

"You got nothing else on anyone?" he asked, turning his attention back to his own partner.

She sighed. "Gabby was born and raised in Hawaii. I assume she can swim pretty good since, you know, she grew up on an island and all."

He scowled at her completely baseless and snippy reply.

Living on an island had nothing to do with swimming ability. Just as being a SEAL didn't mean he loved the water. He didn't.

He'd rather run every day over having to swim. He truly hated both swimming and the ocean. But he did it all and he'd done it well. He just didn't enjoy it.

But even so his being in the water today for this race would be preferable to Shelly being in there. He'd trade places with her if he could. And he knew not to bother asking because there was no way they'd let him.

If they would let them trade off, the two married SEALs from the other shows who had a relationship with the producers would have already done so.

"Being able to swim and swimming a mile in the surf off this island are very different." Stefan hoped Shelly didn't find that out the hard way today.

"Since I've got nothing to tell you about them, do you have anything to tell me about how to not lose this race?" she asked.

Or not drown, he mentally added to her question.

It was a delicate dance he did between making sure she understood the very real danger and scaring her so badly she froze up or refused to compete at all.

"Stay far away from the rocks so the surf doesn't throw you against them. And be careful walking barefoot to the water. Some of these cactus needles will penetrate a boot. If you get cut, the blood will attract sharks."

Terror widened her eyes.

Okay, maybe that last part had been too much information for her. That was his bad.

He dismissed his prior comment with a wave of his hand, hoping to lessen its effects. "Don't worry about sharks. They'll go for the sea lions first."

She visibly swallowed and started to look a little pale. He decided to keep any further advice to himself.

"Five minutes. Meet up at the rally point. We're starting the race early." The kid who acted as Shelly's assistant had trotted up and delivered that news before scooting away.

Shelly reacted accordingly, her nerves visibly ramping up to danger levels as she watched the kid leave then spun to look at Stefan.

"Good thing we never got around to eating breakfast," he said for lack of anything else helpful.

Swimming a mile with a full stomach in frigid ocean water was not a good idea. In fact, it was downright dangerous. Cramps were a very real possibility.

Apparently, no one in charge cared about that because the race was about to begin. And during the coldest part of the day when the sun hadn't had time to warm up the sand or the water yet.

Were these producers masochist or just stupid? He decided to find out.

"Stay here. I'll be right back." He didn't wait around to answer the question from Shelly that would no doubt follow his announcement.

He took off running in the direction Jonas had gone. He caught up with the kid easily and grabbed his arm. "Hey. Can I talk to you?"

Jonas glanced around, as if unsure. Like he was looking for someone to ask permission. Finding no one, he said, "Um. I guess. Sure."

Stefan was firmly in favor of doing what he needed to do and asking forgiveness later rather than taking the time to obtain permission before, so he said, "Why is the race happening this early?"

Jonas audibly swallowed. After what felt like a long moment of hesitation, he said, "I guess it's okay if I tell you… We got a report of a storm moving in. We have to get the race in before then."

Even an impending storm would increase the roughness of the surf. He could hear the waves crashing on the beach, on the rocks. Loud. Violent. And these guys were going to throw seven females of questionable experience and skill into the drink with a storm coming in?

"No. Cancel. Postpone. Do the race tomorrow."

"We can't change now."

"Why not?" By all indications the producers were making things up as they went along. They could do whatever the hell they wanted to.

"Money. We've already got extra cameramen on the clock out there on rented boats to film the race.

"Shit." He bit out the cuss. "This water is dangerous."

"I know."

"Do you?" Stefan asked.

Jonas nodded. "I've got a buddy who just went through BUD/S. He told me some stories."

"And you're going to let these women go out there anyway?"

Jonas pressed his lips together. "I'm not in charge."

Frustrated, Stefan huffed out a breath. "I hope whoever is in charge doesn't regret it."

He spun on the sand and stalked back to their campsite where Shelly had listened, mostly.

She'd waited there for him, but she was up on her feet,

pacing. And she'd changed into her swimsuit. He could see it beneath her T-shirt.

A one piece, thank God, and not some sexy bikini she'd lose all or part of in the surf.

"Any chance they're going to provide wetsuits for the swimmers?" he asked.

That wouldn't help with the rough water, but it would keep her warmer and keep her from getting scraped up.

One big wave crashed extra hard against the shore. Like an exclamation point punctuating the unspoken danger of the Pacific before a storm.

"I don't know," she finally answered, her fear clear.

"Let's go find out." When she didn't move, he reached out and took her hand. "It's going to be okay."

She looked as if she didn't believe him. He couldn't blame her. After one final squeeze, he gave her a little tug then released her hand and strode toward the rally point.

When they arrived at the circle of strategically placed logs where they all sat for group filming, he stopped and breathed in relief. Each log had a wet suit laid out. Along with short swim fins, goggles and an open water buoy to be strapped onto the swimmer for safety so they could be located easier in an emergency.

Feeling slightly better about this swim, but not much, he said, "Come on. Let's get you dressed."

19

"I never wore a wet suit. Or fins," Shelly admitted.

Of course, she hadn't. Because why would she have?

Stefan scowled. It was just one more thing the producers of this show should have thought of before scheduling this challenge.

"Don't worry. I'll help you."

Getting into a wet suit could be challenging.

Getting someone else into one was even more so. Especially when that someone had soft curves he shouldn't be touching as he helped her yank it up her body.

One inch at a time he wrestled the tight suit up one leg, then the other. It was slow going. Not to mention embarrassing for both of them as he tugged two fists full of fabric between her thighs.

"I—I can do it." She reached for the fabric and he hissed as she dug her nails into it.

"Stop. Your nails… Just let me do it."

He finished with her legs. But there was still her shapely hips and ass. And her tits. Jesus.

He glanced up and saw she was red faced. "I'm almost done."

She drew in a breath. "Okay."

He worked it up her arms, making sure the suit was pulled up onto her shoulders enough so it didn't restrict her motion.

Covering her arms seemed no less invasive or personal than when he'd done her thighs and crotch area. Maybe that was because he was so close to her face. Close enough to hear her breaths. See the individual lashes framing her big blue eyes.

Then there was the breast situation.

He drew in a breath and said, "Bend forward at your waist."

After a quick surprised glance, she did as told. "This position shows where there is extra fabric that needs to get pulled up your body," he explained so she wouldn't think he was a pervert.

He grabbed the folds in the stomach area and started to work it up her chest region, cursing himself for offering to help in the first place. Cursing her for having nails long enough to puncture the suit so she couldn't do this herself.

"Put your fins on as close to the water's edge as you can

because you're going to have to walk backwards over the sand once they're on your feet." He started to spew facts at her as he worked on the suit. "Once you are in the shallow water, you can turn around and walk. Lift your knees higher than usual until you're in water deep enough to swim."

She nodded but looked a bit shellshocked from the information overload. That couldn't be helped. There was a lot to say and not much time to say it.

Everything he told her, what little advice he could offer at this point with no time left, was critical. Although, if he was honest, he talked as much to distract himself from her body as to inform her of what she needed to know.

"When you're swimming, the motion is like a flutter kick, which gets tiring the longer you do it so don't depend just on your legs. The fins will help double your speed, but you'll still have to use your arms."

"Okay," she said, still looking dazed as he tugged on her suit.

Damn, this was taking forever to get her into this thing. Best that he continue his instructions.

"Start out slow. You don't want to cramp up. That'll kill you—uh, your time." He did a verbal dance to cover the truth he'd almost spilled. That a bad cramp out there in the deep water could prove deadly.

There was one more danger he couldn't ignore.

"If you get caught in a rip tide when trying to get back in, *don't* fight it. You won't win. Swim parallel to shore until you're out of the current then aim for the beach."

If she wasn't developing a tan from all the time they'd been out in the sun, she would have been white as a ghost after his coaching speech. Great.

But at least the hard—and embarrassing—part of getting her into the wetsuit was done. He moved behind her to deal with the still open zipper.

Damn she looked good in the suit. Like *Sports Illustrated* good.

He ignored that—mostly—as well as the close proximity of her shapely butt as he leaned close and used both hands to zip the neoprene. Just in time too. No sooner had he finished wrestling Shelly's disturbingly sexy body into the wet suit did the show hosts arrive.

Clay and Tasha on site were a sure sign that things were about to get moving.

Of course, the cameras never left. Twenty-four/seven they were there. Watching. Listening.

Usually they kept in the background so he almost—almost but not quite—forgot they were there. But sometimes they were right in his face, like now.

They must have brought in extra crew for the race. There seemed to be double the number of cameras.

Stefan had managed to ignore the camera who was circling them as he struggled to dress Shelly.

Now, it was less easy to ignore the lens in his face.

Annoyed by this show—more than he usually was—he stared right into the lens and said, "Do you fucking mind?"

That should ensure the footage ended up on the cutting

room floor. Good. That would serve the producers right for putting the contestants in danger.

Risking his life for BUD/S was one thing. Risking Shelly and the other contestants for ratings was inexcusable.

Rage had him inside a bubble of self-righteousness that was popped by the sound of Tasha's voice.

He lifted his head and spotted her. She was smiling as usual next to Clay who was stone-faced as per his default expression.

Both were camera-ready and beautiful in matching billowy off-white outfits. They wore what Stefan would call, for lack of a better term, *casual beach wedding* attire. Probably designer.

He was rocking the *beach bum* look himself. Wrinkled cargo shorts. A T-shirt the show had provided that had his name printed on the back. Sneakers, because there was too much shit on this island for him to step on to go barefoot.

And unlike him and Shelly, he'd bet Clay and Tasha had a full breakfast in their bellies and were both on their second cup of Starbucks too. Not that they needed the fuel to just stand there and say a few sentences. They weren't about to dive into the ocean and be pummeled by storm waves.

"Hello!" Tasha began with an enthusiasm that only angered Stefan further. "It's challenge number two today and I know I'm excited to see how it all plays out. Clay? What about you?"

Tasha smiled and spun to face the SEAL next to her, who looked taken off guard by the question.

"Uh, yeah," he replied, covering for his surprise over her obvious ad lib from the script. "So... today is the ocean swim. One mile in the surf that surrounds San Clemente Island."

Tasha took over again to say, "Swimmers will start on the beach. When the horn sounds, they'll run, or waddle in their fins, into the water and swim straight out to the first buoy. Then they'll hang a right and swim to the second buoy. There they'll turn back and make their way back toward the shore where they began."

"The team comprised of the last swimmer back and her SEAL coach will be eliminated," Clay finished.

"We'll get started in just a few minutes once everyone is suited up. Contestants, are you ready for today's challenge?" Tasha shouted.

"No," Shelly breathed out barely audibly.

He glanced at her then reached out and covered her hands with his. "I'll be right there with you."

She met his gaze. For a second it felt as if they had a connection as her eyes and his locked. Then she snorted out a laugh. "Yeah. On the *shore*."

She pulled her hand out from under his and used it to push off the low log as she stood.

Brushing her hands together to knock off the sand, she said, "If I die—or end up in the hospital in a coma—please send somebody to get my cat out of my apartment so she doesn't starve to death. I only left her enough food and water for a week."

He would have smiled at the morbid joke, but he didn't think she was kidding.

"You'll be fine," he lied.

Her blue gaze met his again. "Let's hope."

After a big breath in and then out again she grabbed her fins and turned toward the water.

He followed, realizing he'd forgot to tell her she had to warm up. Getting her into the wetsuit had been challenging but it didn't qualify as a warm-up.

"You need to get your muscles warm," he said.

"How do I do that?"

"Do some jumping jacks."

"Seriously?" she asked, looking like she thought he was joking.

"Seriously," he confirmed.

"Okay." She breathed in and started.

"Do about twenty of those then pull your knees up to your chest a few times and then stretch out your arms like this." He demonstrated as she watched.

While she was busy doing his quick on the spot warm-up, he glanced behind him and saw emergency medical personnel gathered and tried not to think that a bad omen. They'd been here for the run too. Probably a mandate from the insurance company.

As the oppressively heavy, moisture laden air felt thick around him he turned back to stare at the water.

Gone was the blue of a clear day. Today they were enrobed by shades of gray. The colors of a storm.

The ocean and the similarly colored sky melded together, making the line of the horizon nearly indiscernible.

White-capped waves crashed onto the rocks and the sand. Loud. Angry. Frightening.

She was a good swimmer, he reminded himself. Then called bull shit on that statement. He didn't know that. Not for sure.

A summer swim team during middle school. That meant nothing. Was she nuts? Were the producers?

With a renewed sense of panic and doom he turned to survey those around him. He found the SEALs she'd told him were the stars of other network shows standing nearby.

"Keep going. I'll be right back."

She didn't look happy at his announcement but he took the few steps across the sand to join the other SEALs anyway.

"I don't like this," he spat out when he arrived.

The younger one, Nick, shook his head. "Join the club."

The blonde one, Zach, breathed in deeply. "Gabby will be okay. She's a strong swimmer."

"Well, I'll bet you not all of them are." Stefan swept an arm at the group of women standing by, waiting for the horn to blow. "And it doesn't matter. There's a storm coming in."

Nick glanced up. "Yeah. Maybe. It does look like it. Feels like it too."

"No maybe about it. They moved the swim to the morning instead of later today because of a storm."

Zach's gaze finally left Gabby and shifted to Stefan. "This is a fact?"

"Yes!" Stefan confirmed. "One of the assistants told me."

"Shit." Nick scowled and looked to his friend. "What do we do?"

Finally, they were listening to him. Thank God. He might not have any pull with this production company, but their show stars should.

Zach's features hardened. "We grab Joanne and demand they postpone this."

Nick shook his head. "I haven't seen her today. I don't think she's here yet. It's early. She usually gets here later in the day on the first boat."

"Then we grab Clay. He'll throw his weight around and make them cancel." As Zach spun toward the group of production people, the horn blew.

20

At the sound of the starting horn, Stefan pivoted toward the shore.

He saw Shelly was lined up along the water's edge amid the other six swimmers. He hoped she had strapped her fins on tightly enough as she turned and backed into the water as a few of the other swimmers flopped their way there forward.

Stefan breathed out a curse. Giving up on the hope they'd cancel the event, he pivoted to plan B—making sure Shelly didn't die.

He barely registered as the cold water hit his bare feet. He took another step forward and the force of a wave hitting his calves nearly cost him his balance.

It was impossible to stand where the waves broke. He retreated back to the shore and turned back to locate Shelly in the water.

She'd made it past the break. All the swimmers had. It

was hard but he spotted her in the group, her stroke staggered at first as she fought against the waves until she got past them.

The first buoy was too far, in his opinion. He knew that one mile out the depth was nearly four hundred feet and he'd guess the first buoy was a good five hundred feet from shore.

The swimmers would still be in deep water out that far. And they'd remain in deep water while swimming between the first and the second buoy. That portion of the swim made up the bulk of the mile. Then they'd turned back to shore and their starting point, forming a triangle pattern when they were done.

All in all the swimmers would be in the water for over half an hour, possibly closer to an hour for the really slow swimmers. How many of them could handle that?

This was hardcore shit. Not as tough as real SEAL training but too hard for the average person. Especially since their preparation time had been about twelve hours and his training with her consisted of not much more than a pep talk.

That there were multiple boats on the water didn't relieve his worry. The boats were there for the camera crew, not for water safety.

In fact, unless he missed something, it looked as if there were no lifeguards on site at all. What the fuck?

They'd be on their own if anything bad happened. He should have demanded there be SEALs in each of the boats as well as on the shore. If they were going to play lifeguard for this race, they needed to be where the swimmers were.

He squinted into the distance, trying to distinguish between the swimmers as they got farther away. He cursed his lack of binoculars. Then he cursed this insane race and this whole damn show.

Stefan had never felt more helpless than he did right now, standing on dry land and worrying while watching Shelly getting tossed by the ocean.

Even out past where the waves broke the water was rough. Turbulent enough to cause swimmers to experience seasickness. There were a few SEALs in his BUD/S class who, during the five-and-a-half-mile swim, got sick enough they'd puke and then just keep swimming.

Open water swimming was no joke. And no place for an amateur. Yet there they were—seven of them. Out there at the mercy of the sea.

He bit out a curse and paced a few feet forward before retreating back.

Did no one have binoculars? He took his eyes off the swimmers long enough to scan the crew and the other SEALs. He didn't see binoculars, but he did see a camera. And it had an extraordinarily large lens.

He stalked to the cameraman. "How much can you zoom in with that lens?" he asked.

"You're not supposed to talk to me."

Fuck the rules. "Answer the question," he bit out, leaving no doubt he expected an answer.

"Pretty close," the man finally answered.

"Are any of the swimmers in trouble?"

The cameraman let out a snort. "They're all bobbing around so much I don't think I'll be able to tell if they're drowning or just trying to make headway against the current."

The same was probably true for the crew out in the boats. If they weren't trained in open water swimming, they might not notice a swimmer in trouble.

Stephan cussed again. That was it. He was ending this insanity. He kicked off his sneakers, pulled off his socks and T-shirt and ran for the water.

"What are you doing?" Zach called to him as he passed the SEAL.

"I'm going in," Stefan yelled back without stopping or turning around.

"Are we allowed to do that?" Nick asked.

"Fuck *allowed*." He didn't know or care if the SEALs or the camera caught that comment.

He was Shelly's coach. If it was *against the rules* to coach her from inside the water, it shouldn't be.

SEAL candidates trained with a swim partner. The producers should have had them in the water to begin with. And when he heard he wouldn't be, he should have insisted.

Even though it was far from his favorite part of his SEAL training, he was a strong swimmer. But without swim fins, it was taking him longer to get to her than he would have liked.

He reached the first of the swimmers. He passed the

slower ones while cursing his lack of goggles as he did his best to locate Shelly.

Finally, he spotted her.

She'd just gotten hit by a cresting wave and had taken in water. He swam to her side and touched her shoulder.

Bobbing in the water, she spun to look at him as she choked.

She took a second before she coughed out, "Stefan?" The goggles were obscuring her vision.

"You're okay. A lungful of water is scary. I know. Can you go on?"

She nodded.

"Good. I'm going to swim alongside you. Okay?"

"Yes." Her reply was breathless and followed by a cough.

"All right. Follow me. I'll set the pace." He'd keep it slow and steady and adjust as necessary if she started to fall behind.

Just his presence seemed to calm her. They got into a rhythm as they swam parallel to the shore.

They were probably equally matched at this point. She had the wetsuit keeping her warm and buoyant. He did not. She had swim fins. He did not. She had goggles. Again, he did not. Not to mention he was being weighed down by his water-soaked cargo shorts.

All and all, it was a shitty swim—almost as torturous as anything the instructors had come up with during his training— and he hated every damn minute of it.

He was aware of the boat and camera crew nearby and

barely resisted the urge to give them the finger for putting them through this.

One mile. That was all he had to get through. He found himself employing the same techniques he'd used in BUD/S. One stroke at a time. Then one more. Don't look ahead. Just get through this one moment in time. Then the next.

The water was never warm here, but at least it wasn't deadly cold this time of year. He most likely wouldn't get hypothermia from not wearing a wetsuit for this mile. He hoped.

Fucking show.

His head chatter ceased when they reached the second buoy. And though the longest stretch of the swim was over, the hardest part was still ahead of them—getting back to shore without being bashed into the rocks by the increasingly rough surf.

He turned toward the shore. Shelly followed, changing direction.

About twenty strokes in, he felt it. The rip current fighting him. Pulling him out to sea, away from shore, no matter how strong a stroke he used or how hard he kicked.

Fuck.

He lifted his head and found Shelly. She was struggling too, already exhausted after a swim she was ill-prepared for.

They should have been training for this show—for all of the insane challenges—for at least the past month. Not thrown into them on no notice to fill a hole in a schedule.

His anger fed his adrenaline as he reached out and touched Shelly. She stopped trying to fight the current and lifted her head.

As they both bobbed, he pointed for them to keep following the line they'd been swimming in until the buoy and said, "Rip tide."

She nodded, hopefully remembering his advice about swimming parallel to shore until clear of the current.

He was about to follow Shelly when he noticed a couple of the swimmers nearby struggling. He couldn't leave them there like that. It was dangerous. Deadly. Insane.

With one more glance at Shelly, who seemed to be clear of the current just a few yards away as she turned toward the shore and swam freely, Stefan worked to get to the struggling swimmers.

It looked like for the moment he was coach to a few more. But that was by far preferable to being part of a search and rescue, or search and recovery if he didn't help them and the worst happened.

Fucking show.

21

Stefan wasn't swimming beside her any longer. She dared to break her stroke and look behind her, trying not to panic. He was way back.

She couldn't wait for him. Her muscles were tired and getting more so. Even just treading water now was exhausting as the grey water churned around her. Tossing her at will.

The knowledge that the ocean bottom was far, far below her and the shore even farther away was enough to have her heart pumping faster than the swim had.

One stroke at a time. Wasn't that what he'd told her? Aiming at the shore, she dipped her head down and began the slow steady rhythm. Repeating in her head with each rotation of her shoulder, *one stroke at a time*.

The suit was starting to chafe her in places she hadn't considered.

The rough ocean made it almost impossible to take in

a breath of air without also getting a gulp of water in her mouth.

It was physical torture like she'd never experienced. This was the closest she'd ever come to truly understanding why Stefan complained about BUD/S so often. She'd never discount what he said again.

The thoughts kept her mind occupied, maybe too much. Before she knew it, a wave had taken her and she was heading for the rocks barely visible above the roiling water.

She tried to change her trajectory. To navigate away from where the wave tossed her.

It was too late.

She hit hard as the wave tumbled her. She was aware of the pain in her shoulder as she struck the hard surface. Then her hip. Then her head before the blackness closed in.

The sensation of someone very close was the first thing she was aware of even as her eyes remained closed. She could hear their breath, fast and labored as she was jostled against something hard. A body maybe.

She realized that she had been airborne when she got the feeling of someone laying her down on the sand.

"Get the EMTs!" a voice yelled.

"We need a stretcher!" another voice demanded.

Everyone sounded so agitated. Why were they all so upset?

She decided to open her eyes and find out. But when she did, she could barely see.

Panic set in until she realized it was the goggles she still wore.

Lifting one hand she tried to push them up and off her head.

The first person she saw was Stefan, leaning low over her as he kneeled on the sand.

"Thank fuck." Stefan breathed out in obvious relief.

He lifted his head and glanced around.

"She's awake," he announced. "We still need the medics over here. She's probably got a concussion."

"I'm fine," she protested as she saw the ambulance crew running toward her, the requested stretcher between them.

Jonas leaned low. Concern etched clearly in his features. "Are you okay? How do you feel? You hit the rocks pretty hard."

He looked especially worried about her well-being. A small part of her wondered if it was concern over a friend and coworker or if he was just imagining the paperwork nightmare ahead of him if she weren't okay.

"I think I'm okay," she answered as one of the emergency medical technicians shined a light into her eyes.

"Can you follow my finger?" the female EMT asked.

Shelly did as told, hoping she did it well so they'd leave her alone.

She didn't like being the center of attention on a good day. But to be the star of the footage the editors had probably already ear marked in their minds to feature on *the most shocking episode of the season* was even worse.

The camera was right there over her, blocking out what little sunlight filtered through the cloud cover. They didn't want to miss getting even a second of her unfortunate incident.

Stefan was still there close by too, but for a different reason. She guessed it was guilt as he kept repeating, "I'm so sorry, Shell. I'm sorry I wasn't there. I *should* have been right there next to you."

Still woozy, she didn't respond to his apology. Instead, she tried to sit up, then regretted it as she felt muscles she'd never been conscious of protest.

"You really should stay laying down—" The second EMT, a guy, said.

"No," was all she said in response. She was fine. She'd just gotten knocked around a bit.

There wasn't blood or anything. Wait. Was there blood?

She reached up and gingerly felt the lump beneath her wet hair. She drew back her hand and glanced at it. Nothing red or even pink.

In light of that good news, she struggled to sit again.

"Wait. Slowly. Let me help you." Stefan leaned low over her and slid one arm beneath her back.

He smelled of the sea—although she supposed she did as well.

She tried to help by bracing her hand on the sand but found her arms were like rubber from the long swim.

He reached down and looped her arm around his neck. "Hold on to me."

His skin was warm even though the drops of water still beading off his hair felt cold as it fell on her.

This close she could see all the various flecks of color in his eyes. She felt the soft brush of hair on his chest against her bare arm.

Up close and personal with his two day's growth of stubble she imagined how rough it would feel if she were to rub her cheek against it.

He cradled her in his arms as she sat between his legs. She wouldn't have minded closing her eyes and resting for a bit. Her limbs felt like lead. Her mind too as thoughts moved slowly.

She deserved a nap after that swim.

Joanne's voice had her drooping eyes widening.

The woman herself appeared amid the crowd gathered around her. "How are you?"

"Fine," she answered without thinking.

"No. Not fine," Stefan bit out.

"I am tired and sore, but I'll be fine by tomorrow after a good night's rest." On the ground. In a tent.

Ugh.

But if how hard she slept after the run was any indication, she'd sleep well tonight after that swim.

"You were knocked out cold. You could have a concussion," Stefan began.

"Do not say I can't go to sleep because of that. I'm fine." And tired as hell.

"You heard her. She's fine." Joanne turned to find the cameraman right there and took a step out of the shot. "We ready to shoot the elimination ceremony?"

Stefan let loose a string of obscenities so creative she had to smile.

Once he was done with his tirade, she said, "Help me stand?"

"You sure?" he asked.

"Yes." They weren't going far anyway. Just to the meeting area where she'd happily sit on a log and not move for a little while.

The camera followed every motion as Stefan helped her stand and then supported her as she walked.

"You okay?" Dani asked as they moved past where she stood looking as water soaked and exhausted as Shelly.

"All good. You?"

"Regretting saying yes to this show but yeah, all good." Dani nodded.

Next to Dani, Nick looked less forgiving, but she couldn't worry about keeping the cast happy. Let Joanne deal with any issues since she was here.

Right now, the need for self-preservation was strong. Shelly was fine with allowing herself to take off her associate producer hat and just be a contestant.

Stefan helped her sit on what had become their log, guiding her down while supporting her weight against him. He was treating her like she was especially delicate and breakable, which she was pretty sure she'd proven wasn't true by bouncing her way to shore and living to tell about it.

Once she was sitting and had decided she wasn't going to fall over, he still didn't let go. He left one arm wrapped around her.

"Do you need anything? Water?"

"Maybe in a bit." Her stomach was still woozy from the ocean water she'd swallowed or the concussion she was going to deny having.

Eyes focused on her, Stefan moved her hair so he could inspect what she suspected would be a colorful bruise by tomorrow on her forehead.

Zach approached holding his wife's hand. Gabby looked as exhausted as Shelly felt, though less battered.

"Hey. Stefan, is it?" Zach asked, with a very masculine lift of his chin in Stefan's direction.

Stefan glanced up at the SEAL standing nearby. "Yeah."

"I saw what you did out there. I wanted to say thank you," Zach continued.

Stefan sniffed. "Why are you thanking me? Your wife was doing great. She wasn't one of the swimmers I had to help."

Gabby took a step forward. "No, but I saw you guiding the others, so I knew to avoid the rip tide before I got caught in it. So thank you."

He tipped his head. "You're welcome. And good race. I saw you pull ahead and win."

She looked a bit shy as she said, "Thanks."

When Gabby and Zach had moved away, Shelly tilted her head to get a better look at Stefan. "You helped the other swimmers?"

"Yeah. Just a little. I showed them where to go to get clear of the rip tide. I waited until they were all past it. And I know it's a competition and I shouldn't have, but I couldn't leave them out there—"

Shelly shook her head. "No. Of course you couldn't leave them out there. I'm glad you helped them. You were right too, about the swim challenge. This was too dangerous. We shouldn't have planned it."

"Wait. What are you saying? I was right?" He drew back in mock shock as he joked, "You definitely have a head injury." Then he sobered. "I should have been there for you, Shell. Helping you get back safely onto shore should have been my only priority. You getting hurt is my fault."

"No. I should have waited for you. That's what swim buddies do. Right?" she asked.

"You're right." He smiled and in it she thought she saw respect. Maybe even admiration.

The dynamic between them seemed to have shifted. Was this change temporary, brought about by his guilt over not being there when she'd crashed onto the rocks?

She didn't know and didn't have time to figure it out as Clay and Tasha and the camera crew started to set up.

"Shit. They're back," Stefan grumbled.

"You know no day ends without the elimination

ceremony and the announcement of tomorrow's challenge."

"I can't wait to hear what fun we'll have tomorrow." He scowled.

"Fucking land navigation," she mumbled.

The schedule was ingrained in her brain. The land nav in particular because it was the last challenge on the island before they moved back to civilization.

Stefan broke into a wide smile, drawing her attention back to him.

"What?" she asked at his strange glee over her comment.

"I like when you cuss." He leaned closer and added softly against her ear, "And I love that you're starting to hate this fucking show as much as I do."

She didn't confirm his last statement, but she didn't deny it either.

And she really wasn't ready to admit, not to herself or to him, that his whisper had sent an electric current through her body. That the shock of it had awakened certain parts of her that had gone from dormant to demanding.

When her gaze dropped to his lips, so close to her as they sat, the image of her kissing them flew into her brain.

Sometime between meeting him and now, annoyance had turned to attraction. Hate had turned to heat.

If they were alone, if they were anywhere other than here and now, she'd be kissing those lips. She'd let him peel off her wetsuit. Let him do things to her body for days.

And, as movement in her peripheral vision brought her attention to the camera zoomed in on her and Stephan to catch every little nuance between them, she realized she was in big trouble.

22

Land navigation took advance preparation, training and precision.

It was not just getting dropped off in the middle of nowhere and finding your way home, as Shelly had guessed it was yesterday after the challenge was revealed.

After the trauma of the swim, Stefan had let her hold on to her delusions. He figured he could burst her bubble in the morning after letting her get as peaceful of a night's rest as she could with the wind and rain battering their tents.

Well, morning had come and with it a sunny new day, and now was the time.

He kicked dirt over the fire he'd built to boil the morning's water and ducked into the flap of her tent.

She was hiding out of sight inside the tent to enjoy the instant coffee and instant oatmeal he'd procured for them, while the other contestants were still suffering with whatever weird shit the show had provided for breakfast.

He knew she wasn't wearing even a drop of makeup since they weren't allowed to bring any personal items, yet she somehow managed to look amazing, even given the crude living conditions.

Yesterday's swim had meant her tresses dried into soft sexy waves. Being in the sun so much had added highlights to her already blonde hair and had given her skin a healthy golden glow.

She'd been pretty before. She was distractingly more so now.

He dragged his eyes and mind off her, staring at the floor of the tent as he said, "We need to get started on the land nav training as soon as you're finished eating."

"What can you teach me?" she asked. "The sun rises in the east and sets in the west? I already know that."

"That vast knowledge is not gonna be all that helpful to you," he said, sliding the strap of the canvas bag off his shoulder.

"What's that?" she asked, eying the new addition to their meager belongings. Eyes widening, she hissed, "Did you rob the base again?"

"No. This is courtesy of your assistant, Jonas. Who asked how you were feeling, by the way."

She let out a snort. "No doubt. The show's lawyers are probably worried."

"Now, now. That's awfully cynical of you."

"Just call me Cynical Barbie."

He grinned before sitting down and getting to the lesson. "We have here a compass, which is why you don't need to watch the sun, a topographical map, and a protractor and a pencil, both for drawing lines on the map."

Glancing up he saw her staring at the items skeptically.

"Questions?" he asked.

"Not yet but I'm sure there will be."

So was he. He was good at navigating himself, but teaching someone else to do it? That was a whole other skillset.

Best they get started right away.

"So when they drop you off, you first have to figure out where you are. You do that by putting the map on a flat surface along with the compass. Find magnetic north on the compass. Turn the map until the north line on the map matches the compass. Then you have to look around you for any prominent nearby land features, then find them on the map. Then you place the compass on the terrain feature and draw a line back to the vantage point. Understand?"

He glanced up from the map he'd been demonstrating on and got his answer by the glazed look in her eyes.

"Um, maybe we should try pacing first," he suggested.

"What's that?" she asked.

"You need to determine how many paces—steps—it takes you to cover one hundred meters. By knowing that number you can always calculate how many paces the distance you need to cover will take."

This time her eyebrows rose high. "There's math involved?"

That comment stopped him in his tracks. They hadn't even gotten to azimuths and triangulation yet.

It was going to be a long day and, no doubt, a long hike for her.

At least the crew had cameras with night vision, according to her. They probably used it to spy on the cast and catch them being naughty. But if worst came to worst and the sun set before the women got back to camp, the SEALs could use the night vision to plan a night rescue and find their missing teammates.

Hero SEALs to the rescue. The viewers would love it —and he hated with every fiber of his being that he'd even thought that.

This show was changing him and he feared it was not for the better.

Shelly had changed him too. Or maybe it was just his feelings for Shelly that had changed. Because many hours later, he found himself pacing as he waited, worried, for her to return.

"Relax, man. What's with you?"

Stefan lifted his head to find the guy who was partnered with the marathon runner. He was short and stocky, but strong and muscular. Tony was his name, or something close to it. And nothing seemed to bother him.

"I'm wondering where the girls are. It's getting late."

"They'll be back when they're back." Tony shrugged.

Nick and Zach had been conferring together and joined them now.

"Sunset's coming on soon," Zach informed them all unnecessarily.

"When do we call this thing and go out looking for them?" Nick asked, glancing around the small group.

Tony shook his head with a snort. "I'm not going anywhere. The crew can go get them."

Zach and Nick, both married to their partners, frowned at Tony.

He wasn't married or even close to it with Shelly but Stefan felt and shared their rage at Tony's nonchalance.

The sound of fast footsteps and underbrush crunching underfoot heralded the return of the first contestant. And of course, it was Tony's partner, running at full speed to the rally point even though no other contestants were in sight.

"Told you not to worry." Tony grinned as he stood to go congratulate his partner.

It was encouraging that at least one of the women had returned. And hopefully the rest weren't far behind, but a little empathy on Tony's part for the men whose partners hadn't returned would have been nice.

"I'll go with you if it comes to that," Stefan offered, turning toward Zach and Nick.

Zach nodded. "Thanks, man. I'll let you know if and when we head out."

Jaw set, Nick nodded. "And Clay told me he and

Tasha have been getting choppered in. If we have to, we'll commandeer that bird for the search."

Stefan liked how Nick thought. And liked even more how their search and rescue plan was coming together.

Hell, why wait for sunset. They should go now before it got dark.

He was ready to go tell Jonas they were taking things into their own hands when noise caught his attention.

The footsteps, accompanied by laughing and chatter got louder. He turned toward the sound in time to see three females come into view—Shelly and Nick and Zach's wives.

He spotted Shelly, the tallest and the only blonde in the group, easily enough.

Zach and Nick ran to their wives and were greeted with hugs and kisses.

Stefan saw Shelly's gaze sweep the beach. When her eyes landed on him, she lifted a hand in a wave. He lifted a hand in response. It was hard, but he held back and waited for Shelly to come to him.

"Hi," he said when she finally arrived.

"Hi." She smiled. "I made it."

"I see. How'd that happen?" He tipped a chin toward the two women she'd appeared with.

"Gabby and Dani were already working together. I happened to meet up with them at one of the check points so I joined them."

"And what if you three got back last? Who'd lose?" he asked.

"That wasn't going to happen. We saw Backstabbing Barbie heading to the final checkpoint while we were heading back." Shelly's gaze dropped away before she brought it back to meet his. "We might have kind of told her to go the wrong direction."

His eyes widened.

"That sounds horrible. I know." She shook her head.

He smiled. "She'd have done the same to you."

"Well, I didn't tell you this, but during the run for the first challenge, when we were on the final leg, she pushed me out of her way to pass me on the path. Hard enough I fell into the brush."

"You could have been hurt." Stefan's eyes narrowed. "And I helped her through the rip tides during the swim."

"I know. It's okay. You did the right thing helping her in the water. And I was fine on the run. I caught myself on my hands. I only got scraped up a little. But I am going to credit Karma for putting us at the right place at the right time on the course today to intercept her." She smiled.

Noise announced the return of another contestant.

They all turned in time to see Model Walk Barbie emerge from the path, holding her side as if she'd run the last part of the course.

She'd earned her name for always strutting as if she was in front of a camera, which to be fair on this show she was. But she wasn't walking like she was on a runway now as she stumbled to a stop.

Stefan grinned at Shelly. "That's all of them, *except* for one."

More noise was punctuated by a female voice cursing up a storm.

He turned and saw Backstabbing Barbie having a hissy fit when she counted the females on the beach and realized she was the last to return.

Gabby and Dani each shot Shelly a thumbs up and a grin.

He watched Shelly visibly work to control her smile. He didn't bother controlling his.

After learning what she'd done to Shelly on the run, for once he was going to enjoy the elimination ceremony. Immensely.

23

"Ah, and so we have returned to the place we met." Stefan grinned as Shelly arrived on the obstacle course early the next morning.

"So it is." She forced a smile, dreading this day. And the upcoming challenge.

His gaze zeroed in on her, as if he could tell something was off. "How'd you sleep?" he asked.

"Fine." It was her go-to answer that worked for almost any question. Especially when she wasn't telling the whole truth.

"You must have been happy to have a bed."

"And a shower," she added.

Not to mention a toilet. All seemed like luxuries after camping on the island. The accommodations base command had arranged for their use at the Navy Gateway Inn were surprisingly nice.

"You must have been happy to be back home," she said.

He nodded. "We got in so late last night, the guys don't know I'm back yet, so it was a peaceful night. Tonight won't be. Once they figure out I'm home they'll be all over me asking questions."

She compressed her lips. "Remember. No—"

"No revealing winners or losers of the challenges. Non-disclosure agreement. Yada, yada, yada." He leveled a less than patient glare on her. "I know."

"Okay. I trust you." It was herself she didn't trust. The upcoming challenges were going to test her even more than the first three had. "So, fast roping…"

He nodded. "Let's hit the tower."

The four-story high tower that was usually used for the rope slide had been repurposed for today for them to use for the fast rope challenge.

Four stories. She swallowed hard. She'd been so worried about the parachuting that she hadn't considered the height required for the fast rope challenge. Height equaled bad in Shelly's book.

"Clay and Tasha said the clock starts from the moment you start the climb up the tower and ends when you hit the ground again at the bottom of the rope." Stefan walked as he talked. "I figure the speed of the climb is what's going to win or lose this challenge. The rope itself is nothing."

Nothing to him. To someone with a fear of heights the tower, the rope, this entire course, was terrifying.

Everything seemed high. The wall. The cargo net. And especially the tower climb and rope slide.

The closer she got, the heavier her feet felt. Her heart pounded until she felt lightheaded, and she hadn't even left the ground yet.

There were other teams already there practicing. It seemed they all had the same idea as Stefan. Get an early start before the sun got too hot and get as much practice in as possible before the challenge.

She could use that to get out of practice. "Um, there's already people here. We can wait."

He glanced at her. "We'll take turns. They'll be too tired to go right back up again. There's plenty of time for everyone."

The shaking started with her head as she disagreed with him, but involuntarily spread to her whole body until she was trembling and woozy.

She squatted down and let her head hang to try and avoid passing out.

Stefan was immediately beside her. "What's going on? Are you okay? Is it your head? Fuck. I knew we should have taken you to the hospital after you hit your head during the swim."

She felt the warmth of his large hand on her back. It should have been comforting. In the shadow of that four-story tower, it wasn't. Nothing would be.

"I don't want to let you down—"

"What are you talking about? You're doing great. You said so yourself, you don't have to win. Just not lose."

She shook her head. He didn't understand. She wasn't worried about losing. She couldn't do this at all. Couldn't go through with today.

There was no way she could climb that tower.

It was good she was going to have to tell him now—better that they dropped out now—instead of making it all the way to the final challenge and having her frozen in fear on the high wall.

She shook her head. "I know you want that money—"

"Do you want to know why I want that money?" he asked. "Yeah, at first I thought I might like to put a down payment on a house, but I looked online and prices have gotten insane so I probably wouldn't have done it anyway. What I really want to do is send my parents home to Poland. They haven't visited since before I was born. And my sister has never been. We have first cousins she's never met. That's why I really wanna win."

"Aww. That's really nice." And it made her feel even worse she couldn't get it for him.

The guilt on top of her fear was too much. Her vision blurred from the tears she couldn't hold back.

"Shit. Come on. Come with me." Stefan grabbed her arm and tugged her up and into a standing position before he pulled her away from the course.

"Where are we going?"

"To my Jeep where we can have some privacy. I think we need to do some mental training before we start with the ladder and the rope."

He still thought she'd be able to do the challenge. He

hadn't figured out yet that she was trying to tell him she couldn't. That she quit. That he wouldn't even have a slim chance to win because she was a quitter.

Where was that bell when she needed it? He might understand she was quitting if she rang out.

Picturing his disappointment when she finally got through to him had her tears turning into sobs, which turned into hiccups once he had her situated inside his vehicle.

"Jesus. Shell. It's okay."

"No, it's not."

Hiccup.

He let out a sigh and she felt his arm snake around her.

"Come here." Getting as close as the vehicle would allow, he held her tight, using both arms to capture her against his hard body. "You're going to be okay."

"No. Not—" She sucked in a stuttering breath. "—me. You."

Hiccup.

He pulled his arms from around her to cup her face, forcing her to raise her head and look at him. "What are you trying to say?"

Didn't he understand? She wasn't worried about her being okay. She was worried he wouldn't be after she dropped out and made him a loser.

"I can't—" She was such a wreck she couldn't even tell him what she couldn't do. "—disappoint you."

He waited for her to continue, his dark eyes close and intense as he focused on her. Then those eyes narrowed and his gaze dropped to her lips before coming back up to meet hers.

"Shell."

Her lips parted on a breath. "Y-yeah?"

His mouth hovered close. So close it would take barely the slightest movement on her part to close the distance.

It turned out she didn't have to move because he did. He covered her mouth with his in a kiss that began slow but quickly became intense.

She reached up and grabbed the back of his neck. He angled his head and deepened the kiss, his hands grasping as he ran his palms down her sides to hold her hips.

Then he stopped himself, breaking the kiss and pulling his hands away.

There was something that looked like regret in his eyes as he said, "I'm sorry."

She shook her head. "It's okay."

At least the shock of the kiss had chased away her hiccups and stopped the sobs she hadn't been able to control on her own.

He looked like he didn't believe her as he drew in a breath and blew it out before meeting her gaze. "Look, if you're trying to tell me that you're afraid you'll disappoint me if you lose, don't worry. I won't be. You've done great. And even if you didn't do this challenge at all and decided to just quit and walked away from this whole thing, I still wouldn't be disappointed in you. Or mad. Or upset. I promise."

His words, amazingly, helped.

Now that the pressure was off, she felt a tiny flame of determination spark to life inside her. "No. I'm not quitting. I'll try."

"You sure you're good?"

She nodded. "Yes."

Apparently just one kiss had made her crazy, but she was going to do it. Climb those four stories and slide down a rope. For him. God help her.

Meanwhile, he was visibly excited at her decision. "Okay. I'll be right there with you the entire climb up and on the platform with you. I won't let you do this alone."

Their eyes met with a deep, intense gaze. "Okay. I trust you."

He looked as emotional as she was when he said, "Good."

24

He'd kissed her.

She'd been hysterical crying and what had he done? He'd freaking kissed her.

And now they both had to get their head in the game and get her up that tower and down again in one piece, without her having another nervous breakdown.

The prize money was on the line. Not to mention, he just plain didn't like to lose.

He still wasn't sure what had her hysterical in his Jeep. She'd bounced right back after her accident during the open water swim. She'd handled the other two challenges just fine.

What was it about this—

As he watched her hands shake and her progress slow to a crawl it became clear.

It was the height. She was afraid of heights. It was so obvious. He should have seen it before.

He drew in a breath. Now that he knew, he could at least try to do something about it.

Grabbing the ladder, he began to climb until he reached where she clung, all forward motion at a halt.

"I'm right behind you."

She moved to look down at him.

"Don't look down. Keep your eyes on the rung ahead of you. One rung at a time. Okay? Slow and steady. Only concentrate on the next step up the ladder. Nothing ahead. Nothing behind. Got it?"

"Y-y-yes."

Shit. She sounded nearly catatonic.

"I'll be with you the whole way."

"O-okay."

If she was so damn afraid of heights, why did she plan a fast roping challenge? He guessed the answer as he waited for her to slowly advance to the next rung. This must have been Jonas's idea.

He needed to have a talk with that kid.

Hell, maybe he should go straight to the top and talk to the big boss. Was that this Joanne person they all tiptoed around?

He had a lot of time to think and consider the situation since Shelly was moving at the speed of a three-toed sloth. And he couldn't blame her. He'd overcome a fear or two during BUD/S.

Hello, drown-proofing.

He was at a loss as to exactly how to motivate her by using his own experiences on this very course.

Should he tell her that as candidates they had to climb up the platforms without aid of the ladder, so she should consider herself lucky? Would that be helpful? Probably not.

Above him, Shelly drew in a big shaky breath and let it out.

Uh, oh. He figured that was the O-course equivalent of a death rattle. Her prelude to ringing out. Her final breath before she gave up and they had to tie a harness to her and lower her to the ground.

He was formulating an inspirational pep talk, a last gasp effort to help his partner get through this, when she began moving.

Fast. Climbing the ladder like a woman possessed.

He didn't know what had gotten into her, but he wasn't going to question it. She reached the first platform and kept going without slowing down.

They passed the second platform and were on the way to the third when he called up to her, "Stop and stand on the next platform. You'll access the fast rope from there."

She didn't answer but did as he'd said.

By the time he pulled himself up onto the third of the four tower platforms she was waiting. Pressed up against one of the support beams far from the edge, but at least she was there and upright.

That would have to be good enough for a start. Now to get her to the rope and down to the ground.

With his dreams of that prize money fading fast he moved to her. "You all right?"

She nodded. It was a quick stiff movement of just her head that made her look like she was in a back brace. He needed to shake her up a bit. Get her out of her own head.

He pressed her face between his palms. Her eyes, the same color as the sky that surrounded them, met his as he leaned close. "You can do this. I'm gonna do it with you."

She swallowed hard and gave him another tiny, terrified nod.

"What got into you that you started climbing so fast?" he asked, unable to control his curiosity.

"I just wanted to be done."

He raised a brow. "Good. That's the attitude. And guess what? The hard part is done. Now is the easy part. You'll be on the ground in a few seconds. You just have to get down that rope."

That didn't seem to pacify her.

"You want me to go first and you follow me?"

That elicited an energetic head shake. "No. Stay with me."

"Okay. I'll go behind you then. Keep your eyes on the rope. Don't look up at me. But know that I'll be there right above you."

They fast roped in secession as a team. All they needed was a yard or two between them to make sure the guy on the ground got clear before the next guy hit bottom.

Of course, with the speed—or lack thereof—with which Shelly moved, there was a good chance he'd be hanging up there on the rope for way too long just waiting for her to go.

He handed her the smaller of the two pairs of gloves he'd grabbed from the box the production crew had left at the bottom for them to use.

After pulling on his own pair and watching her pull on hers, he repeated what the instructors had ingrained in him years ago, "Strong hand. Weak hand. Hook the foot. Turn and go."

He reached for the rope, pulling it to him where he stood on the platform to demonstrate the technique for her while repeating the command, adding, "You're going to let the rope slide through your gloved hands. You can control your speed with your foot and knee pressure against the rope."

Still holding the rope with one hand, he said, "Your turn. Repeat the command back to me."

She inhaled a shaky breath and repeated what he'd said.

"Good." He nodded and thrust the two-inch thick rope toward her. "Now do it."

Her eyes held millennia of accumulated human fear of falling. Of death. It was a lot to conquer in one morning's training. He was going to give it his best anyway.

"The sooner you get down, the sooner it will be over." When she didn't look convinced, he added, "You only have to do this twice. Once now. Once for the competition. After that, you never have to do this again."

"Not true. The full obstacle course is the final challenge."

Shit. He mentally reviewed every obstacle she was going to freeze on and realized there were a lot. That was going to be fun.

He'd cross that bridge when he came to it. He had to get her through today first.

Meanwhile, that she'd told him one of the future challenges, something she'd refused to do before, was proof of how scared she was.

He schooled his expression to not reveal his surprise at her revelation and lifted one shoulder. "Who says we'll make it to the finals? Pfft. I'm thinking Marathon Barbie is a ringer. Probably black ops. She's gonna win it all anyway."

Her lips almost twitched into a smile before fear pulled then into a thin hard line again.

"Okay." She reached for the rope. It seemed even thicker in her smaller hands. Glancing at him she said, "Strong hand…"

"Strong hand, weak hand," he confirmed.

She grasped the rope and stared at the edge of the platform for long enough he wasn't sure she'd be able to bring herself to go over it.

Finally, she moved. Hanging on for dear life with her hands she hooked her foot, turned and dangled. Hanging there, not moving, but on the rope.

"Now go. The ground is waiting for you. And I'm right behind you. Just loosen your grip just a little."

She slid down a few feet with a squeak.

"You got it. Keep going," he shouted in encouragement, moving to the rope as much to watch her as to be in position to go down himself.

She yelled her way all the way down. The kind of scream you heard at theme parks from people on the roller coaster. Part terror, part thrill. Then she was down, shakily standing at the bottom with a death grip still on the rope between her hands and legs.

More teams had arrived. By the time Stefan made it down to her, her friends Dani and Gabby had Shelly in a group hug.

Zach and Nick stood nearby offering verbal praise.

"Good job up there," Zach said when Stefan approached.

Stefan nodded. "Thanks. It was touch and go for a while."

"So we saw." Nick cocked a brow up suggestively and Stefan had a feeling he was talking about more than Shelly's struggle with the rope.

"She going to be up to do this again for the competition?" Zach asked.

Stefan blew out a breath. "God, I hope so."

25

She could do it. She'd done it once already, Shelly reminded herself.

Just one more time then that was it. She could stay down on the ground where it was safe...until the damn parachute challenge. Then the obstacle course challenge which would put her right back up here on the tower of terror.

Don't think about that. One trauma at a time.

She didn't have to be the fastest today. And chances were good she wouldn't be the slowest either.

It turned out Model Walk Barbie, who'd just gone before her, had no upper body strength. Her slow struggle to climb the ladder put her way behind everyone else's time who'd gone before.

Shelly would be the last contestant in this challenge. Not a bad place to be. She knew what time she had to beat. And if she plummeted to her death, at least they had the footage for the day already shot before the police shut the set down.

In the most shocking episode of the season, tragedy strikes…

Pushing that morbid thought out of her mind, she pulled herself up onto the platform and fought the light-headed sensation the height caused.

Stefan wasn't up there with her this time. He was right below, waiting for her down on the ground. She glanced down to find him and the reality of the height hit her. Hard.

She froze, wasting precious time she should be using doing what he'd told her.

What was that again? Right hand, left hand? No. Strong hand, weak hand. Or was it weak hand, then strong hand?

"Shell! You got this." Stefan's firm, loud voice seemed as much a command as an encouragement.

It was enough to knock her out of her stupor.

"Here goes nothing," she said to herself aloud since no one else was there to talk to.

She tugged on the gloves that Stefan had tucked into belt and reached way out to grab the rope, realizing how far it was. Last time he'd handed it to her.

Swallowing hard, she leaned out over the abyss, planted her hands and feet on the rope, and down she went, sliding fast until her hands felt the heat through the gloves.

She wanted to slow down. She wanted this to be

finished more. Before she knew it her feet hit the ground and then her butt until she was sitting on the sand still clinging to the rope between her legs.

It didn't matter. She was down. She was safe.

With a whoop, Stefan was next to her, hauling her up and against his hard body. She was so happy this was done, she threw her arms around his neck, then jumped up and wrapped her legs around his waist.

He spun them around but she was already dizzy so it didn't matter. "You did it! And you beat Slow Poke Barbie's time."

She was giddy. Laughing while clinging to Stefan. Riding an adrenaline high.

Then she noticed the cameras. More than one, closing in around them. Circling them like sharks.

She unwrapped her legs from around him as he set her down. Once her feet hit the ground the two of them quickly broke apart.

Glancing behind her, she found Clay and Tasha, along with the rest of the cast and crew.

"Where are we doing the elimination ceremony?" she asked, like she hadn't just been climbing Stefan like a monkey up a tree.

Like she hadn't been ready to do a whole lot more with him.

She glanced at him now and saw something in his eyes. Desire?

What did he see in hers? Desire or mania? Probably mix of both.

"We're going to meet up by the start of the course," Jonas finally answered her question.

"Good. Good. Let's get this done." She nodded and glanced back at Stefan. "Coming?"

He drew in a breath and bobbed his head. "Yup."

She barely made it through the elimination ceremony without reaching out to touch him.

He stood close to her. So close she could feel the heat radiating off his skin. So close, he could probably feel her body vibrating.

It barely registered when Tasha and Clay announced the next challenge for the following day—sharp shooting. Easy. It didn't entail her leaving solid ground so she was good.

Then it was over. Her responsibilities for the day fulfilled. Work was done. Time to play.

She turned to him and waited for him to say something.

His eyes tracked the cast and crew moving towards the parked vehicles. "You, uh, came in the van?"

"Mm, hm."

"I can give you a ride… if you want me too."

"Yes, please." She wanted him to do much more than give her a ride in his Jeep.

He'd barely slammed the door of the vehicle when she jumped him. All it took was one look. His eyes meeting hers, the need clear in his gaze.

She wanted sex. Judging by that look so did he.

Her lips crashed against his and he parried by

grabbing her ass in both palms and dragging her into his lap.

The steering wheel was in the way. She hit the horn by accident and the loud beep had him pulling back from her mouth.

His eyes were heavily lidded and his breathing rapid as he said, "I'm not supposed to bring any females into the bachelor barracks."

That was not a problem in her eyes. She didn't want to think he had women in his room on base anyway. "I'm staying at the Navy Gateway Inn."

His lips bowed into a smile. "Let's go."

They tumbled into her room the minute she got the door open, tearing clothes off as they went. She pulled off some of her own, then reached to tug off some of his.

She was sandy and worried she stank from the cold sweat of fear and nerves.

He didn't seem to care as he tossed her onto the bed and pulled off the last of her garments.

Her sports bra and underwear hit the carpet along with the T-shirt, tactical pants and boots the show had provided.

Then his underwear hit the floor. She'd seen him without a shirt during the swim and had managed to not make a fool of herself over his amazing body then. But Stefan completely bare and in front of her was enough to wipe her mind of all else except for him and what they could do together. What they were about to do together.

He crawled onto the bed and laid on his side next to

her. His gaze locked onto hers as his roughened palm slid down her body before he glanced around the room, including up at the ceiling. "There aren't cameras in here, are there?"

She hadn't thought of that, but she wouldn't put it past Joanne. "Not that I know of. Want me to check?"

He shook his head, sweeping his gaze down the length of her bare body before he brought it back up.

On a groan, he moved over her and said, "I'm starting not to care."

As she felt the weight of his body on top of hers and the hard length between her legs, she had to agree.

26

He was a morning guy. When other guys moaned and groaned when the alarm went off, Stefan would already be up and out of bed.

But this morning he had no desire to leave this particular bed. And that was solely because Shelly was in it next to him. Soft, warm, and naked.

He needed to get back to the barracks. Shower. Change clothes and get to the shooting range for that day's challenge. Who knew how much training Shelly would need for this one.

But since he'd woken at the crack of dawn, there was time. He didn't have to go just yet.

And it would be a shame to waste such an eager morning woody.

With a groan he nestled up behind the curve of Shelly's ass as she lay on her side facing away from him.

That put his hard length comfortably at the apex of her thighs. Right where he wanted it to be.

He nuzzled her hair, moving to her ear where he nipped on a lobe before traveling down to kiss her neck.

She groaned, a sound that was likely a protest over his waking her. But when he slid his hand over her hip and down her belly to between her legs that sound changed to a definite moan of pleasure.

He smiled and slipped a finger between her lower lips, teasing her open for him.

Knee bent, she invited him in, and he accepted the invitation gladly.

Sliding into Shelly for the third time was no less amazing than it had been the first two times the night before.

They fit together like they were made for each other. She responded to his every touch, which only made him want to touch her more.

He worked her with his hand while her body gripped his length inside her and he knew he'd never get enough of this woman. That thought should have scared him. As she came and he drove himself to completion inside her, it didn't scare him one bit. Not even close.

His good mood didn't waver even after she kicked him out so no cast or crew would see him leaving. He had things to handle anyway before the day's challenge began.

He reached his room on base and realized he was starving. They'd never actually gotten around to eating dinner last night. They made do with peanuts from the mini bar between round one and two in her bed, but only after he'd confirmed the production company would be footing the overpriced bill for them.

The refrigerator in his room yielded better than expected. He'd forgotten he'd frozen some of the pierogi his mother had sent last. He could do way worse than his mother's homemade pierogi for breakfast.

They were better fried in butter with onions and served with sour cream but desperate times…

He tossed the food from home into the microwave instead and stood by impatiently watching the time count down.

Of course, he couldn't get away with being in his room without at least one of the team noticing. The aroma attracted them like sharks to blood in the water and moments after the microwave dinged there was a knock at the door, followed by the door opening because Stefan hadn't bothered to lock it.

Raising his gaze from where he sat at the lone table in the room hunched over his plate he saw Eric aka Thor darkening his doorway.

"Hey." The man wasted no time striding across the room where he reached out and poached one of Stefan's eight prizes.

Stefan pulled the plate back to protect the remainder and shot a glare at the man. "If you are here just to steal my food you can leave. I have to get to the shooting range within the hour and I don't have time to stop and get something else to eat."

"When you gonna be done with this show?"

"A few more days, I guess. Why?"

"Because we're, uh…" Eric's hesitation drew Stefan's complete attention. The man drew in a breath and finally said, "We're getting spun up."

"When?" Stefan asked, his chest tightening.

Eric shrugged. "Tomorrow maybe. The next day latest. Hell, could be tonight for all we know. You know how it goes. We're all packed and just waiting for the call."

"Fuck." Stefan bit out the curse as he pushed his plate away.

"Can you get out of the show?" Eric knew what Stefan was thinking and what had him losing his appetite.

He wanted to be with his team. He should be with them on that transport.

"I don't think so. They've got me tied up in some contract."

"Command should be able to get you out of that," Eric said.

"Command is the one who made me sign it." Stefan scowled.

"Listen. Don't worry about us. Five operators are plenty. Besides, we're meeting SAS and who knows who else over there."

Stephan drew his brows low at that information. "NATO?"

Eric dipped his head in a nod.

"Ukraine?" Stefan asked.

Eric paused just a beat, but it was long enough to tell Stefan the other man was debating how much he could and couldn't say.

They couldn't even fucking tell him where they were going if he wasn't going with them.

Finally, Eric said, "No. But not far off."

Fuck. Stefan stood and paced to the window.

"It's okay. We're good to go without you."

Eric might have meant that to make Stefan feel better but it only made him feel worse.

He spun to face the man. "You shouldn't have to."

"None of the guys blame you."

The team didn't have to blame him. Stefan had that well covered. He was already blaming himself.

Danny leaned in the open doorway. "You're back."

Stefan held up one hand to avoid a repeat of the conversation with Eric. "Just to change clothes. I'm on my way out."

Danny grimaced at that info before he focused his eyes on Eric. "Team meeting in ten."

Eric nodded. "On my way." Then he glanced at Stefan. "Represent, brother. You dominate that competition. We'll see how you did when we get back."

If they got back.

Stefan pushed that uncharacteristically cynical and dark thought from his brain.

Not being with his team was messing him up. But he had another teammate waiting on him. The one who had spent a good portion of last night crying out his name as he made her come.

What a difference an hour made. He'd gone from feeling the highest of highs to the lowest of lows.

When the guys were gone, he showered quick, changed his clothes and tried to rally his spirit to finish this thing.

If he was going to do this show, he would do it right. If this damn show was going to keep him off an op, he was going to at least make sure his team dominated the field. Just like Eric told him to do.

He tried to keep his spirit up but by the time he walked onto the shooting range, it was waning fast.

Shelly was already there, suited up in protective gear and practicing.

He stopped a distance behind her and squinted downrange. She was a good shot. He could see that by the paper target she'd already punctured with six rounds.

When she noticed he'd arrived, she put down the weapon, took off her ear protection and turned to peer at him through the safety goggles.

"You can shoot?" he asked, not hiding his surprise.

"I used to go to the range with my dad before I moved away from home. He's a cop."

He hadn't known that about her. He frowned. "You're not from here?"

"God, no. I'm from Ohio. I came here for college and then got a job after graduation." She laughed. "Is anyone really *from* California? Most everyone I talk to moved here for something or another. Judging by that accent, you're not from here either. New York?" she guessed.

"Brooklyn," he confirmed.

There was a lot he didn't know about her. A lot he wanted to learn. But right now, his heart and his mind weren't in it. They were with his team, possibly rallying to board a transport he should be on at this very moment.

"What's up with you?" She pinned him with a narrow-eyed stare.

"Why do you ask?"

"I can tell something's wrong." Suddenly, her expression clouded. Her perfectly shaped brows drew low. "Is it because of *what happened*?"

She'd mouthed the final words silently as her gaze shifted to see who was around them. It reminded him that they were being listened to and filmed, which he seemed to have forgotten.

As miserable as he was, he didn't want her to think that he regretted what had happened between them. Nothing could be further from the truth.

Last night—and this morning with her—were the sole bright spots in his current gloomy mood.

"No. God, no. It's, uh, work." He didn't know much, but he could tell her even less than what he did know.

Everything the SEALs did was classified. But if they were going to be in *that* region, operational security on this mission would be even more critical.

"The team's getting spun up," she said as more of a statement than a question.

His brows shot high as much at the accuracy of her guess as her choice of wording.

"How do you know that term?" he asked, without answering her question directly.

Her gaze dropped away. "I've been watching old episodes of SEAL Team on television. I thought it might help with the show."

Still looking embarrassed by her confession, she finally brought her gaze back to meet his.

He managed a small smile. "Anything for the show, right?"

Anything—including watching his brothers fly into harm's way while he played commando for the cameras.

"You want to go with them," she guessed correctly yet again.

He sighed. "Doesn't matter because I can't. Can I?" he asked.

Could she pull off some miracle and get him out of his contract?

She shook her head. "Barring a physical injury that will take you out of the competition, you're legally required to participate in every episode's challenge until we get eliminated."

He snorted. "For the first time since this clusterfuck started, I'm kind of hoping you lose."

She narrowed her eyes as if she were trying to see inside him. Hell, maybe she could.

He'd tried to perk up. Fake it 'til you make it. But he wasn't that good of an actor. If he were, he'd be living in a mansion in the Hollywood Hills instead of in the bachelor barracks in Coronado.

Shelly could see he was down in the dumps, which is probably why she looked so confused when she said, "I thought you wanted the prize money."

"Some things are more important than money." He let out a short, wry laugh when he realized the truth of that statement. Perhaps he was growing as a person.

"That's very philosophical of you," Shelly observed.

He tipped his head to the side. "Eh. I have my moments."

She drew in a breath then glanced at the gun. "Would shooting the hell out of some paper men help cheer you up?"

He blew out a snort. "It couldn't hurt."

27

"You think Marathon Barbie can shoot?" Shelly asked, eying the competition through the annoying safety glasses as the woman in question and her SEAL teammate strutted by.

She figured Gabby and Dani would be pretty proficient with firearms since they were married to SEALs.

That left the uber competitive woman also known as Stone Faced Barbie and her partner Tony as the only wild cards in today's challenge.

Stefan put his cell away after glancing at it for the dozenth time and raised his gaze. "I wouldn't doubt anything about that one."

Shelly had to agree.

Old stone face probably did triathlons for fun in the off season when she wasn't running marathons. And what was that Olympic winter sport where they were on cross country skis and then had to shoot targets in the woods in between? She probably was a gold medalist in that event.

Stefan sighed, again, and glanced around. "When do you think we're starting?"

"I don't know. I can ask," she offered.

"It doesn't matter." He shrugged.

He was miserable and though he hadn't told her much, she knew why. The evidence was all there. The malaise. The constant checking of his phone. His team was going on a mission without him.

If *SEAL Team* had taught her anything, it was that guys didn't like to be left behind. And, more importantly, any change to the team dynamic could put the welfare of the team in jeopardy.

At least, that's what happened on more than one of the episodes she'd binge watched.

Joanne would never let Stefan out of his contract. She'd loved him for the cast from day one. And she no doubt had him primed to be the most popular character on the show.

What Shelly had told him was true. He was required to participate *until* they were eliminated. After that, Joanne would want him at the finale. And she would no doubt make sure he was called back as a coach for the obstacle course challenge by the finalists to give him more airtime.

But, if he was already gone—and gone because he was in service to his country—what could Joanne do? Sue him?

It would be very bad optics for the show to not support a hero off risking his life while protecting our freedom.

What was that old saying? *Better to ask forgiveness after the fact than permission before.* This seemed like one of those times. Suddenly she knew exactly what she had to do.

"Five minutes," Jonas said, popping his head into her little shooting cubicle.

"Thank God," Stefan breathed out, obviously itching to get going even though she could see his mind was elsewhere.

Her heart pounded as the full ramifications of the decision she'd just made hit her. She could get in trouble, but only if they could prove what she'd done. She'd just have to make sure they couldn't.

The shooters would take turns so the camera could fully capture both the competitor and the reaction of the opponents as each shot either hit or missed the mark.

Shelly leaned out and yelled to Jonas. When he came back she said, "Can I go last?"

"Um, yeah. Sure." Overworked—and she knew from experience, underpaid—Jonas didn't have the time or energy to question her request.

That was exactly what she'd been counting on.

"Thanks." She smiled. Now she'd know what score she had to beat. Or rather, miss by.

She watched the others more closely than ever before.

Gabby sucked so badly that even her loving husband

covered his eyes at one point rather than see she'd completely missed the target with one of her shots.

Marathon Barbie was good, as expected. But not good enough to win. Judging by the scores, she'd come in a solid second.

Dani was the ringer. She hit every shot with precision perfection. She was so good her score got a round of applause from the cast and the crew.

"How the hell did she do that?" Stefan asked no one in particular. Even in his misery, he'd paid attention to her shooting.

Jonas was hovering behind them since Shelly was shooting next. He answered, "She goes to the range regularly with Nick for stress relief. She said it's either that or axe throwing." Jonas shrugged and turned his attention to Shelly. "You ready?"

"Ready." She nodded and turned to pick up the gun and check her ammunition.

She'd already calculated what she had to miss, and what she could hit to make it look like nerves had hit her and not like she was taking a dive.

She glanced at Stefan one last time. His nose was in his cell again. He glanced up and saw her looking at him and pocketed the phone.

"You good?" he asked, forcing himself back into coach mode.

"Yeah. All good." She turned back and faced the target. And proceeded to lose the challenge, perfectly and with precision.

The cast was dead silent as Jonas announced the score and they realized it put Stefan and her out of the competition. There was a polite round of applause for them as the couple about to be eliminated.

She accepted it with a tight-lipped nod as she glanced at Stefan. "Sorry."

His confusion was clear. So was the moment it hit him what she'd done. His eyes widened and he grabbed her by the arm, pulling her away from the group.

Hand still in a vice grip on her arm, he leaned low and hissed near her ear, "You purposely threw that challenge."

She pulled back and opened her eyes wide in feigned innocence. "I would never do anything like that."

He cocked up one brow.

Ignoring the silent accusation, she said, "Call your team. See if they left yet."

The deep breath he drew in expanded his chest beneath his T-shirt, making her itch to run both hands over the solid wall of muscle. She'd just have to remember what it felt like to lie against that chest.

She knew she'd left him a couple of things to remember her by, as well, in the form of hickeys where she'd bitten him as he'd driven her over the edge of ecstasy.

"What are you going to do now?" he asked, concern etching his features.

"Once we're through this elimination ceremony and after you ring the bell—sorry you have to do that—I'll finish up the rest of the show as a producer instead of a cast member." She lifted one shoulder. "No big deal."

"Are you gonna be okay?"

He was most likely asking if she'd be all right career wise. But all she could think about was what it was going to be like finishing up this show without knowing where he was. What he was doing. If he was in danger. Or hurt. Or worse.

She swallowed away the dryness in her mouth and nodded.

Forcing a smile, she said, "I'll be fine."

28

"Talk," Eric said when he answered instead of hello.

"Tell me you haven't left yet," Stefan begged, hoping Shelly's sacrifice wasn't for nothing.

"Tell me you're coming with us," Eric countered.

"I can. I am," he said with a smile.

Eric let out a whoop. "We're in the cages now checking our gear. Wheels up in two hours. Can you make it?"

"Pfft. With time to spare. See you soon." He navigated his Jeep into a spot as the call went dead.

He had to pack and get his own gear ready. But there was a call he had to make first.

Pulling the cell out of the dashboard cradle, he disconnected it from the Jeep's Bluetooth. He navigated to his recent calls and hit to dial his parents' house.

"Another call? What's happening?" Irina demanded.

She was going to grill him again about where he was

and what he was doing. And this time, unlike last time when he'd been lying to her because he wasn't ready to reveal he was on an island filming a shitty reality show, she'd be right. He was heading into danger. There was always a chance he wouldn't return.

"Nothing's happening," he lied. "I'm just going to be busy so I wanted to say hi to Mom and Dad in case I miss Sunday's call."

She was uncharacteristically silent.

"Are they home?" he prompted.

He heard her draw in a shaky breath. "You're going somewhere bad."

"No." Damn. He hated lying. He hated worrying her worse. "Look. I'm going to tell you something and you can't freak out."

"Oh, my God." There were tears in her words.

"I've been cast for a reality show. By the same people who make all those dumb shows you love. The trash and wedding ones."

"Oh, my God!" This time her exclamation was more squeal, filled with excitement rather than fear.

Good. That's how he wanted to picture his sister when he left.

"What's the show? What are you doing? Why didn't you tell me before?"

"Okay, slow your roll, sis. First, I signed an NDA so I'm not supposed to say anything at all. I'm only telling you because I don't want you to worry if I don't call."

"Because they take the contestants' cell phones. I

know. I read that."

"Yup. That's what they do."

"When will it air?"

"I'm not exactly sure. I think one of the producers said pretty soon."

"This is amazing!"

"Yup. Amazing," he repeated with less enthusiasm. "So, Mom and Dad?"

"At the butcher."

"Again? They were just there."

"It's bulk meat sale day."

Jesus. When he retired, he hoped to have more hobbies than just shopping for food. He ran his hand over his face. "Any chance one or both of them took their cell phones?"

"Hang on. I'll look." There was a rustling as she moved. "Nope. Both here plugged into the wall in the kitchen."

He shook his head at his tech adverse parents. "I bought them phones to take with them in case the car breaks down or something."

"Dad's new car has that On Star thing so the car can call for help."

"Fine." He breathed in and regrouped. "Please tell them I love them. And I will call as soon as I'm able. And not to worry if it's a couple of weeks. Okay?"

"Okay! Do good, brother. I'll be rooting for you. I'm going to go search the internet now and see if I can find anything about a new show."

"You do that." He shook his head. "I love you."

"Love you too, bro."

He disconnected and headed inside to grab a few things before he headed to the cages to join his team and get his gear together. Next stop—he wished he knew exactly. But he'd soon find out.

The transport landed safely in Kosovo and they were called directly into a meeting. It was a good thing he'd managed to get some sleep on the plane.

The joint forces commander stood in the front of the small room filled with men. Judging by the array of uniforms and accents there were Brits, who were probably SAS, as well as some French Foreign Legion.

The map on the wall told Stefan a lot even before the man in charge began talking.

"Serbia," he began. "A known friend of Moscow, has just received a care package from China. A cache of anti-aircraft missiles, plus some other deadly goodies."

There were a few low mumbles from the operators in the room after that revelation.

"There are no plans to send in ground troops. But that doesn't mean we're going to sit by and do nothing. Small, covert groups of five to six operators will be performing intelligence-gathering incursions nightly, concentrating mainly here and here."

The commander tapped the map to indicate the

borders between Serbia and the NATO-friendly nations most in danger of invasion—Kosovo and Bosnia.

"We have twenty-one sites of interest. Your recon missions across the border are technically not officially sanctioned by NATO, yet, but there's no time to wait for permission. Reports say Russian mercenaries are already moving into those border regions."

It was clear to anyone watching, the Serbs were slowly, quietly, gearing up for an invasion.

It was straight out of the Kremlin's playbook. Exactly what Putin had done in Georgia and in Ukraine.

And while the world was distracted by the bloody conflict in Ukraine, now would be the perfect time for the Kremlin-backed ally to make a move on its neighbors. Any student of history knew Serbia had been itching to get Kosovo back ever since it broke away decades ago.

Stefan drew in a breath. It was dangerous. Being on an unsanctioned mission meant they'd be on their own, with limited resources. And he was grateful he was there with his team. All thanks to Shelly and her selfless act.

Was she in trouble for what she'd done? God, he hoped she hadn't been fired.

He couldn't help but wonder how far they could have gone if this hadn't happened. If Russia and Serbia had kept their hands off their neighbors' land and he could have seen things through to completion. Not just in the show but with Shelly.

Him thinking of her and the show while on a mission was dangerous. He needed to get his head in the game.

And he would. But when he was home... All bets were off then. She'd be his first stop.

"Memorize the map and the coordinates. We start tomorrow night."

The team funneled out of the meeting room and once they were away from the larger group, Wyatt frowned. "There will be almost a full moon tomorrow night."

"Yup. That's gonna make it interesting to remain covert as we sneak across the border," Stefan added, shaking his head.

"I guess it can't wait. Things are escalating too fast." Mason shrugged.

"Thanks to Moscow and Beijing the fun never stops around here." Eric snorted.

"So we get in, get out, and then we can go home. I'll be buying drinks for some little hottie at McP's before I know it," Ty said with boundless enthusiasm.

"Yeah. After we get in and out *twenty-one* times," Wyatt reminded them of the number of ops the commander had mentioned.

"Well, Rodeo, think of it this way. By op fifteen or so there should be no moon," Ty said.

Stefan shook his head. "No easy day."

The truth was, he didn't need today, or tomorrow either to be easy, but he did need to live long enough to go home. He had a lot to go home to.

In the typical game of sit-around-and-wait they played so often in the military, the discussion of what they wanted to do first when they got back home inevitably came up as they sat and watched the clock for go time.

"I'm going directly to McP's for a drink," Ty confirmed. No surprise there.

"I'm getting a nice hot shower. The showers here suck," Danny complained.

"Hey, Pierogi. What do you want to do when we get out of here? Eat your momma's food?" Wyatt asked.

Eric shook his head. "Hey, we're not allowed to call him Pierogi anymore. Remember? You wanna get punched?"

"Or be forced into a rematch on the O-course?" Danny added. "I for one am tired of running that thing when I don't have to."

After all that had happened recently, that bet on the O-course felt like years ago. And given the task ahead, and the dangers that lay between them and going home, what name they called him seemed inconsequential in the larger scheme of things.

He shrugged, shaking his head. "Whatever. I don't care anymore."

The team stared at him.

Why was that? Just for not caring about a stupid nickname?

What they didn't realize was that he cared very much. Just not about what they called him.

They'd asked what he wanted to do when he got home. There was only one thing.

He wanted to be with Shelly.

29

"Good morning," Jonas said with a smirk that had become part of his usual look around her since about the fast-roping challenge. "Website numbers," he added as he tossed a stack of papers onto her desk.

"Good morning and thank you," she returned without further comment.

She wasn't about to stir that pot.

Yes, she was starting to wonder exactly how much of her and Stefan had been caught on camera and microphone. No, she wasn't going to ask. It would be easier to pretend her private life was private if she didn't know.

They were going to edit the footage to make her and Stefan appear how they wanted anyway. God, she hoped they hadn't actually wired her room to catch them having sex. Her parents were going to see that show. Her friends. Her pastor back home.

This could be bad. Very bad…

"Where is Stefan?"

Shelly was startled out of her misery by Joanne's sudden appearance, not to mention her question.

"Why isn't he in any of the obstacle course footage?" Joanne continued as she filled the doorway, blocking Shelly's exit should she choose to run rather than answer the question.

So Joanne had gotten a chance to review the footage. Shelly had been holding her breath, waiting for the axe to fall, for days. It seemed it finally had.

"Um, Stefan? We were eliminated. In the sharpshooting challenge," she said, avoiding directly answering the question.

"Yes. I realize that. But you knew I wanted him back as a coach for the obstacle course challenge."

Time to come clean. At least partially. "He got called in. He's away on a mission."

She drew her brows low. "Command agreed I had him for the full time. No matter what."

"Yes, but since we'd been eliminated…I told him he could go." She braced herself for the explosion.

"So he isn't in the finale episode either?" Joanne asked, her tone suspiciously even and calm.

"Oh, he is," Shelly rushed to say, before adding, "In the blooper and highlight reel."

She dared to glance up and saw the unhappy line of Joanne's lips.

"I know it's an inconvenience. And not what we

planned. But it was important he go." It might cost her this job, but she had to say it.

The time it took Joanne to draw in a breath and then let it out felt like an eternity. Finally, Joanne said, "Jacob was just called up too."

Shelly's eyes widened at the personal revelation from the ice queen herself.

That confession explained why Joanne had gone missing for the last few days of filming. That she'd missed the parachuting, the obstacle course challenge and the finale had been a mystery until now.

She must have been spending every moment she could with her SEAL beau before he left. Shelly couldn't help feeling envious of that time she hadn't gotten with Stefan.

Even so, she could appreciate how the other woman felt. "I'm sorry," she said, in commiseration.

Joanne visibly straightened. "Comes with the territory. Do you have the website numbers for *Under Pressure*?"

Back to business. Crisis averted.

Now all she had to do was avoid falling into the Stefan-sized hole that appeared in her life when he'd left.

That and make this show a success, otherwise she would lose her job for pitching Joanne a flop. Then she'd have no career and no man.

Sure. Easy. One hit show, coming up.

"Here you go," she said while handing the papers Jonas had just delivered to Joanne.

"How are they?" she asked.

That Shelly hadn't even gotten a chance to look at

them yet didn't matter to Joanne. The woman wanted answers, not excuses.

Going on faith and the fact that when she'd texted Lucy asking about the website she'd gotten a thumbs up emoji back, Shelly smiled and said, "Numbers are good."

Joanne nodded, still looking down at the pages in her hand, which Shelly hoped supported her assessment. Wishing her boss would go, Shelly sat quietly and waited, until Joanne raised her gaze.

"I want you to start thinking about more show ideas."

Shelly's eyes widened. "Oh. Okay. I will. Thank—"

Joanne had already turned and was headed toward her own office before Shelly could finish.

More show ideas. And if *Under Pressure* ended up being a hit, that would be the standard to which any new ideas would be compared. Anything she came up with had to be great.

She blew out a big breath and sagged against her desk chair as she could almost hear Stefan quoting that SEAL motto.

30

The ratings were amazing. They had risen steadily since the premiere of the first episode. The *Under Pressure* website almost crashed after the airing of the swim challenge because so many people were on Stefan's page trying to leave comments.

He was a star. A hero. The show was a hit. Joanne was happy. The network was thrilled.

So why was Shelly so miserable?

Maybe because it had been a month—four fucking weeks—since she'd thrown that challenge and said goodbye to Stefan.

What did that mean? Was he still gone? Was he home and ghosting her?

Had it been a fling? A one-night stand that was never meant to last?

She thought back to the last time she'd seen him. He'd been in a rush to get back to base and to his team.

They'd been surrounded by cast and crew so she couldn't even kiss him goodbye.

But before he drove away, he had promised to call. Was it just one of those things people said whether they meant it or not? She'd thought he'd meant it, but weeks had passed since then and she'd felt every damn day of it to her soul.

His adoring fans didn't miss him. They didn't even know he was gone.

There was a team, led by Lucy, handling the social media for the show. They had someone posting as Stefan, as per the contract he'd signed, which he obviously hadn't read. If he had, he would have objected to having an Instagram account, she was sure. But have one he did. They posted pictures of SEAL-type things and inspirational quotes. He'd hate it.

Too bad for him. He wasn't there to complain.

A text alert sounded from her cell. She dove for the device, just as she had for the past month, only to feel the disappointment when it wasn't from Stefan.

Guilt hit her for feeling like that when she should be perfectly happy to get a text from Alicia. In the past she would have jumped for joy at the invitation to join her best friend at McP's for a drink.

Instead, she typed in a reply. "Thanks. Can't. Working."

It wasn't exactly a lie. She did need to get back to work. Besides the never ending new show brainstorming because Joanne always wanted more, Shelly had been given more responsibilities than ever.

This was her punishment for getting Joanne to notice her and all the great things she was capable of, she supposed.

She turned to her computer screen and couldn't stop herself from scrolling through the latest news. Doomscrolling took on all new connotations now that she was obsessed with everything bad happening in the world as she tried to guess where the guy she'd made the mistake of falling for might have been sent.

As Shelly wasted time she didn't have to spare searching for *current locations of US Navy SEALs* in the browser on her computer, Lucy crept through her doorway.

Shelly frowned at the expression on her coworker's face. "What's up?"

"I, uh, got an advance copy of the sixth episode."

"Okay." Shelly racked her brain to remember which one that would be.

"You and Stefan are uh, featured pretty prominently." Lucy cringed.

Shelly couldn't figure out—then it hit her.

The fast-roping challenge. The day he'd kissed her in the Jeep. The night they'd gone back to her hotel room.

She swallowed hard and asked, "How prominently?" And did she have to ban her parents from watching that episode?

How much had the cameras caught? How much had the microphones picked up?

Oh, God. This was a nightmare.

Before Lucy could answer, Jonas skidded to a halt, grabbing onto the doorway to stop his trajectory.

"I know, Jonas. Episode six," Shelly told him to prevent the horror of having Jonas repeating what Lucy had just told her.

"Stefan's here," Jonas gasped.

"What?"

"He just got off the elevator."

"So why didn't you bring him back with you?" she asked, jumping up from her chair while trying to fix her hair and tug down her skirt all at the same time.

"Because that new intern grabbed him to sign an autograph."

"Great." Shelly rolled her eyes.

A month apart and now she had to compete with the new intern for his time.

"Hey," Stefan said after walking up behind Jonas.

Her heart pounded and her mouth dropped open at the sight of him.

The weeks had taken their toll. He had a month's worth of beard growing on his face and his hair was longer than she'd ever seen it. And he was still the best thing she'd seen in weeks.

"Hi," she said.

"Hey, Stefan. Good to see you. Jonas and I were just

leaving." Lucy practically dragged Jonas away, leaving the two of them alone.

It shouldn't be awkward. She'd done nothing but wish he'd walk through her door for weeks. But now that he was here, she wasn't sure what to do. What to say.

"So the show's a hit," she began.

He laughed. "Is it?"

"Yeah. Actually, it is."

"Joanne must be happy."

"Oh, she is. Also, as you might have guessed, you're a hit too."

"I was wondering what that autograph was about." He hooked a thumb behind him.

"Yeah, the episode of you carrying my unconscious body out of the Pacific broke records."

"Oh, good. I guess." He shook his head and took a step closer. "So, who ended up winning in the end?"

"Nick and Dani."

He dipped his head. "I'm glad. He's a good guy."

"Yeah. They donated the money to a veterans' charity."

Stefan blew out a laugh. "Proving he's a better man than me because I was gonna keep it if I won."

"That doesn't mean you're not a good guy, even though you did say you'd call and you didn't."

"Mmm. Well, you know, the Navy takes our cell phones to keep us off kilter, just like you guys do here with the contestants. They don't let us have clocks or watches either." He took the few more steps to close the distance between them as he abandoned his lame joke and said, "I'm sorry I didn't call. I was hoping a personal visit would make up for it."

"It might," she admitted, not letting him off easy but also wishing he would just hold her already. Kiss her. Tell her he'd missed her as much as she'd missed him.

Instead, he asked, "How did Marathon Barbie do?"

"She and Tony came in second."

"That must have killed her. Losing," he guessed.

Shelly nodded. "Yup. It was kinda great."

He smiled. "I bet."

"Have you been able to watch any of the episodes that aired?" she asked.

As long as he was insisting on talking about the show, now might be a good time to ease him into the idea of what might be in episode six.

"Oh yeah. Sure. The boys and I had viewing parties every week." He rolled his eyes. "No. Sorry. The wi-fi was shit and I figured I could catch up when I got back. I thought maybe I could watch it with you… if you wanted to."

"I'd like that. But…" she began, searching for the words to tell him.

"But?" he asked, no longer looking amused.

"It's not bad. It's not good either," she added.

Brows raised, he silently watched her struggle.

"Okay, I just need you to know that I had nothing to do with it, but I think they've edited our footage to make us out to be the hot and heavy couple on the show," she blurted.

He tipped his head and smiled, surprising her. "Weren't we?"

Her cheeks heated. "Yeah. I guess. You're not mad?"

"No. Why would I be mad?"

"We didn't win, you got no prize money, and now your team is probably going to tease you for the way we're portrayed."

His gaze locked onto hers. "If they want to tease me for being with the hottest, sexiest, smartest woman on the show, then fuck them."

"Aww." Her hardened heart softened at his sweet words.

She decided she'd had enough with waiting for him to make a move. She reached out and laced her fingers with his as she pressed a short kiss to his mouth.

When she pulled back, she said, "The beard tickles."

"Sorry. I'll shave," he promised, leaning away from her.

She pulled him back. "I'll deal with it for a little while longer." She leaned in for another kiss, this one longer and deeper, until a thought hit her. "I forgot. I have a check for you."

"A check?"

"Yeah. Remember? Win or lose, you get a thousand dollars per episode. I managed to get you paid for the finale too even though you weren't there, since you were in the footage we showed of the past episodes. It's probably enough to send your family to Poland. Right?"

"Yeah. It is. Thank you." He grinned and moved in closer. "So, do I get a bonus for being on the record-breaking episode too?"

"What did you have in mind?" she asked as he pressed his body against hers.

"To start, this…" He moved in for another kiss.

She pulled back when a flurry of activity just outside her door caught her attention.

"What's wrong?" he asked.

"There seems to be a camera aiming into my office," she said loudly enough for the people invading her privacy to hear.

"Then let's give them something to talk about." His growly proclamation had need twisting inside her.

He kissed her while backing them up toward the doorway.

There, he pushed the door closed and then flipped the lock before lifting her against him and carrying her to the desk where he sat her on the edge.

He stepped between her thighs and groaned. "I've missed you."

"Oh, yeah? Why don't you show me how much?" she teased in a throaty voice she barely recognized as her own.

He glanced at the ceiling. "Any cameras in here?"

"Do you care?" she asked as she keenly felt every one of the weeks apart from him.

"Not really."

He got down on his knees and pushed her skirt higher while spreading her thighs wide.

Glancing up at her from between her legs, he said, "The beard is going to tickle you down there too."

"I'll deal with it," she said, but those were the last coherent words she managed for the next forty minutes or so.

That was definitely going to give them all something to talk about.

Something to talk about... That actually would be a good name for a new show.

HOT SEAL, COLD WATER

A FUN BONUS SHORT STORY

1

JACOB

It's the simple pleasures in life that make up for all the other bull shit. After thirty-six years on this earth—half of that time spent with a sniper rifle in my hand—I'd learned that, if nothing else.

Things like a second glance from a hot woman seated across a crowded bar. Or a cold beer on a hot day. A thick, juicy, bone-in ribeye blackened on the outside and bloody on the inside. Two weeks leave with nothing to do and the solitude of an empty beach house in which to do it. And, finally, the feel of diving naked into cool, crystal clear water at sunrise.

Currently enjoying the last two items on my pleasure-filled bucket list, I dropped my towel on the deck, climbed onto the diving board and sliced through the water.

After crossing the length of the pool underwater, I surfaced on the other side. There, I turned and pushed off, heading across to where I'd left my towel.

I hoisted myself out of the pool and was just thinking that maybe I'd try to find someplace later today where I could knock off a couple of more things from my list when I heard it. High heels clicking, quick and sure on the stone path that wove through the pristinely landscaped property.

I heard her right before I saw her. And she obviously saw me as I stood there naked and dripping.

Her brows rose and her gaze dropped down my bare body, before she yanked it up to my face and glared. "What are you doing? No one is supposed to be here."

She delivered the accusation with such force and confidence, I almost doubted myself.

Interesting, since I had an explicit invitation from the owner personally and, as far as I knew, she did not. Although I shouldn't be surprised if the old coot had a taste for women half his age. Shapely blondes with ice blue eyes colder than the water I'd plunged into to wake up.

She kept me pinned with her glare as I bent and reached for the towel, but only to wipe my face.

My time in the teams had taught me many things. To be cool in any situation was one of them. To rattle my opponent and knock them off-balance was another.

As I watched her tits rise beneath her tight little top with the breath she sucked in at my action, and my continued exhibitionism, I had a few thoughts. Only one of which was *mission accomplished*. She looked rattled all right and I was enjoying that fact. Probably a bit too much.

It hit me that maybe I should cover up and find out what she was doing here. My absent host, Robert, might be as old as the Hollywood hills but he'd earned his money and his reputation in the picture industry.

The sexy as hell ice queen in front of me looked like she belonged in Hollywood. About as much as I did not.

I took my time rubbing the towel over my hair. My overly long hair, according to my mother. But just right for a SEAL who often needed to blend in and be invisible in foreign countries.

When one dark lock fell over my eye, I shoved it out of the way. Only then did I wrap the towel around my waist, tucking in the end to secure it—although secure wasn't exactly a word I'd use to describe the towel as it rode low on my hips.

She waited and watched. My mystery woman who, honestly, I wouldn't mind getting to know a whole lot better, in spite of her pinched expression.

I let my gaze drop down the tight little skirt that landed well above the knees of her mile-long legs. Yup. She could glare at me all she wanted. I had plenty of other pleasant things to look at.

What had her so pissed at me again?

Oh, yeah. My being here, which was a puzzler.

Maybe Robert hadn't told his paramour I'd be using the place. In which case, I'd better clear this up. And, if she were with him, I'd also better stop picturing her naked.

Paramour? Where the fuck had that thought come from?

I didn't even know I knew the word but somehow I knew with certainty it was the right description for her—*if* she was with Robert in that way. I also knew something else with certainty. Hanging around Robert had changed me. At least my vocabulary.

Folding my arms across my chest, I returned her stare. "I have permission to be here."

"I was told this property was currently vacant." She drew in a breath and let it out in a huff. Lips pressed together she shook her head as she pulled out her cell.

She looked about as angry with whoever hadn't told her I'd be here as she did with me. Poor Robert was in for a reaming if it were him.

There wasn't much I could do about that so I lifted one shoulder. "Sorry. But I'll be out of here in two weeks, if that helps you any."

If my being here was really a problem I suppose I could leave early. Drive back to Coronado and spend the remainder of my leave on base.

Did I want to? Fuck no. Would I, for Robert? Yeah, I would.

We'd gotten pretty damn close over the years. At least, as close as a guy like me could with a rich eighty-year-old retired Hollywood producer who split his time between his beachfront mansion in Santa Barbara and his penthouse in Vegas.

Yup. Robert and I had about as much in common with each other as I did with this woman. But maybe opposites did attract. I sure felt the attraction. Did she?

Hard to tell since she still looked as if my mere presence was ruining her day.

I found the idea of a little anger-fueled sex pretty enticing. What did that say about me? Nothing I didn't already know. That hearts and flowers and romance weren't in the cards for me. Maybe in a few years after I retired, but not now. Although I could hope that a nice hate-fuck was in store for me in the near future.

I watched her rapidly tapping out a message on her phone, which afforded me the opportunity to look at her unobserved. She was probably my age. Although, she could very well be ten years older than me and I'd never know. Such was the magic of modern cosmetic surgery.

Tired of being ignored, I said, "You know, this place is big enough. We could both be here."

In fact, I really liked that idea.

She raised her gaze and delivered a glance that told me what she thought about my suggestion.

"Don't be ridiculous. We're going to need every bedroom for the cast." She shook her head and went back to her cell and I went back to being perplexed.

The cast? What cast?

Was the old man filming a movie here and forgot to tell me?

I reached down for my own cell, thinking it was long past time that I called Robert and asked him what the hell was going on. Then I remembered I was in a towel and my phone was plugged in the wall outlet in the kitchen.

Finally finished with her text, which if I had to guess was filled with all caps and exclamation points judging by her obvious agitation, she glanced up at me. "Look, Mr. —"

I hadn't been called mister in—ever. Master Chief, yes. Mister, no. But I didn't correct her and simply said, "Jacob is fine."

"Mr. Jacob—"

"Jacob's my first name. I'm not formal. No mister necessary." It seemed ridiculous to not be on a first name basis with her. She had seen me naked after all. And I'd been picturing her that way for a good five minutes now. "And you are?"

"Joanne Rossi. New Millennia Media. Out of Burbank. We have a signed contract with the owner of this property and paid her in advance for two months exclusive use for filming starting Monday. And at no time during our negotiations were *you* mentioned." She swirled her finger in my direction, encompassing me and my continued presence.

Joanne. I rolled that name around in my mind for a moment before I focused on the rest of what she'd said and frowned.

She'd referred to the owner of the property as *she*.

Hot Seal, Cold Water

And I knew Robert was due back here next week so why would he rent it out for two months?

I opened my mouth to tell her that when an idea struck. "What's the address of the property you rented?"

She rolled her eyes at me but indulged me enough to consult her cell phone. "One-ten Beach Road."

My lips quirked up. "Yup. That explains it. This is one-hundred Beach Road. The house you want is next door."

Her eyes widened. "No. The GPS said I'd arrived. How could I have—"

"The gates are next to each other and I did notice the bushes are blocking the number." I shrugged.

"I'm truly sorry for intruding."

"I'm not." I grinned.

For the first time since she'd arrived, the tough as nails façade slipped away just a bit and let the woman beneath peek through. "Oh, really?"

"Really." I nodded. "Have you had breakfast yet?"

"I don't eat breakfast."

That might be true but there was certainly a hunger in her gaze as it skimmed over my bare torso. "I bet you drink coffee though," I guessed.

"Yes. I do."

"Then you can drink while you watch me eat."

I swear she looked tempted . . . until she shook her head. "I really can't. I have to get to the house."

"The vacant house that you won't be using until

Monday? Seems like you have time for at least a cup of coffee."

Her lips twitched. "Tempting but I've got a lot to do. I wouldn't be here this early if I didn't."

It was early. Seven if I had to guess.

I would have thought most Hollywood folks rolled in from partying the night before around sunrise. Yet she was here at the crack of dawn beginning her workday. Just one more thing that intrigued me about this woman. The woman who was about to leave, judging by the car keys in her hand.

"Raincheck, then," I said, ever hopeful.

She didn't accept my offer, but she didn't reject it either. What she did do was say, "Thank you for clarifying the address. And again, I apologize for intruding."

"No problem. Intrude anytime."

"Enjoy your breakfast." She sent me an indulgent smile before turning and strutting back the way she'd come.

I shook my head at the tempting view her exit treated me to and the shame she wasn't staying. Then it hit me. I knew where my little intruder would be and when. And I had every intention of repaying the visit.

2

JOANNE

"Good. You're here." Maria, the show's director, greeted me Monday morning as I rounded the pool of the beach house. The *correct* beach house this time.

It was a beautiful property, perfect for our location, but this one didn't come with a hot as hell naked man in the pool.

"The stationary cameras are all installed, both inside the house and outside on the grounds," Maria told me. "The cameramen are here and ready. And the cast should start arriving in the limos in a few minutes."

I nodded. "It sounds like you've got everything covered."

Maria smiled. "This isn't exactly my first rodeo."

"Hmm. Rodeo." That might be an idea for a show. Cowboys were always popular. I tipped my head to the side, making a mental note to check on the most recent ratings of any rodeo airings.

"Uh oh." Maria narrowed her dark eyes at me. "I really need to watch what I say to you or I'll be tiptoeing through cow manure on the next shoot."

"We'll see. We have to get through this one first."

"If this season is even half as exciting as last season ended up, time is going to fly," Maria predicted.

I let out a breath. "We can only hope."

An executive producer was only as good as her last season. That was the double-edge sword of having a huge hit. How to top it?

"The first limo is pulling in." The radio on Maria's belt came to life with that news.

"On my way," she replied before she handed the second radio to me. "Here you go."

"Thanks." I took it and turned, about to follow Maria on her path toward the driveway, when a rustling in the bushes stopped me.

"Good morning." The deep male voice was oddly familiar. When I turned, I saw why.

Temporarily, my mouth fell open, but I was nothing if not quick on my feet. I recovered quickly and took in Jacob, clothed this time. "Good morning. You're trespassing."

"Am I? Silly me. I was out for a run on the beach. I thought I was at the right house. I guess I misjudged. They're so close, it's easy to get mixed up." His hazel eyes twinkled with mischief at the lie.

Meanwhile, I couldn't help but imagine running my fingers through that dark hair . . . and down his ripped abs barely visible beneath the tight, sweat dampened tank top. "I guess I can forgive you this time. Since I made a similar mistake. But you have to stay out of the shot, please."

"Oh, not a problem. I always try not to get shot." He continued to amuse himself. And—dammit—me too. I couldn't help it as my mouth quirked up in a smile I couldn't hide at his corny joke.

I heard the chattering girls and realized my personal and professional worlds were about to collide. "Come here," I whispered loudly enough for him to hear.

One dark brow lifted but he did as I'd requested and moved to stand just behind me. It was then I realized how tall he was. I was five-foot-eleven in my heels. But Jacob still dwarfed me by a few inches.

The four females from the cast didn't even look twice at us as they trotted toward the pool and the bar set up there, stripping as they went.

"Um, what exactly are you filming here?" Jacob asked.

I couldn't blame him. It was starting to look like a porno set as clothes flew and bikinis were exposed.

"It's a new reality show."

"Ah. Interesting."

I glanced back and saw his expression was more amused than interested so I didn't bother explaining the concept. Instead I shrugged. "It's a living."

He nodded, before saying, "So, I'm here for that raincheck. Breakfast?" When I didn't answer right away, he added. "Or lunch?"

"I'm working. It's the first day of shooting."

"Then dinner after you're done for the day."

"I don't think that's a good idea."

"Why not?" he asked.

My kneejerk reaction was to say no without having a reason. I hadn't expected to have to defend my decision. Not that I couldn't. I had plenty of reasons. He was too handsome. Too flirty.

But even if I wanted to ignore all that, there were plenty of other excuses. My job for one. My ex for another and that was all the reason I needed.

"Jacob, I'm flattered. But—"

"This isn't sounding like a yes."

"It's not. But thank you."

"You still didn't give me a reason why."

"I just don't think it's a good idea."

One dark brow shot up again. "It's only dinner, Joanne."

In the sunlight, I noticed the kaleidoscope of colors swirling in the eyes that stayed focused on mine.

"Why are you so intent on getting me to eat with you?" I asked.

"For one, I going to go out on a limb and guess that you're the kind of workaholic who never stops to eat a decent meal. And I happen to believe proper nutrition is very important." He threw that line out as smoothly as a used car salesman. Then he dropped his gaze to my lips before he brought it back up to meet mine. "And, more importantly, I can't seem to stop thinking about you."

I'd been in the business long enough to spot a bull shitter, but that last thing he'd said sounded sincere. And the look in his eyes—it cut straight through me.

I could almost taste his desire. How long had it been since I'd felt wanted by a man? Never mind one as attractive as this one.

I'd sworn off men. Promised myself I'd never be in the position to get hurt again. But I also didn't want to live like a nun at only forty years old.

Three years was a long time to go without sex. Three years was also a long time to still feel the pain of that breakup, but I did. Every time I thought of it. And the only time I didn't think about it was when I was occupied with work.

At least my career was on track, even if my personal life was a train wreck. Maybe it was time to fix that. I sure as hell didn't want a relationship, but maybe it wouldn't hurt to have a lover. Just for a night.

I drew in a breath and realized my heart was thundering. I was never anything but confident at work, but this man, with his pecs of steel that I'd wager matched what I'd glimpsed between his legs by the pool, had me nervous.

I swallowed and said, "We only started rolling today . . . so I won't be out of here until late tonight . . . but, I guess I could swing by your place."

His eyes brightened when he realized, in my long about way, I'd said yes to his invitation. He smiled, slow and sensuous. "I'll leave the gate open and the door unlocked."

He hadn't mentioned food, but I think we both knew I wasn't really going there for dinner.

"You aren't worried about *intruders*?" Nerves had me making a joke.

His grin widened. "I think I can defend myself. And besides, my last intruder didn't work out so badly."

No, it hadn't. But Jesus, when this was over, I hope I didn't regret making a wrong turn into that driveway that day.

3

JACOB

"How's your time at the beach been?" Robert asked while on speakerphone on my cell.

"Eh, it's not Djibouti but it's not so bad," I joked as I stirred the pot of chili on the eight-burner stove in the massive kitchen.

We were eating here tonight because I had no intention of squandering what I feared would be precious few hours with Joanne by taking her to a public restaurant.

Luckily, one of the few dishes I knew how to cook really well would also hold on the stove for as long as I needed it to. Until whenever she arrived. Or until we weren't otherwise occupied . . . Whichever.

"You'll have to tell me about your time in Africa sometime."

"You always ask me to tell you stories, but you, sir, have many untold stories of your own."

"Me?" Robert chuckled.

I snorted. "Yes, you."

Maybe he and I weren't such an odd couple after all.

I knew, from things I'd seen around the house and things he'd let slip in conversation, he had spent time in other places besides Hollywood. A man who had a photo of himself being knighted by Saddam Hussein definitely had a story to tell.

"Hey, did you know they're filming some reality show at the house next door?"

"A reality show? No, I didn't. How do you know?" he asked.

"I, uh, ran into one of the producers. It seems your neighbor rented it to some production company."

"Good God. There goes the neighborhood."

I laughed at his melodrama. "Don't worry. They're only renting for two months then I'm sure they'll be gone."

"Let's hope. Though it would be preferable if they were gone before my return next week."

"I'll see what I can do," I joked.

"If only that were true. I suppose you acquiring some nice tear gas is out of the question?"

I barked out a laugh. "Yes. Most definitely."

He sighed. "All right. Then I guess I'll just see you next week."

"Sounds good. See you then." Still smiling, I disconnected the call.

A flash of car headlights from the driveway turned that small smile into a wide grin.

Happy she'd actually come, I opened the door . . . and was hit with a full body slam. From those long legs to her shapely mouth, she pressed against me.

I recovered quickly enough to wrap both arms around her and kiss her back before this unexpected but most welcome moment was over. I managed a soul-stealing tongue kiss that had me hard as a rock inside my jeans before she pulled away.

"I don't do relationships," she said, her stare pinning mine.

A short, shocked laugh escaped me as she knocked me off balance with the comment. "What a coincidence. Neither do I."

I'd seen what being a team guy could do to relationships, from casual dating to marriages. After growing up in a broken home, I had no intention of trying to start anything serious now.

Although, Joanne's preemptive proclamation made me wonder. What were her reasons?

It was something I'd have to investigate later, because now I was hard enough to drive nails and I had a handful of warm willing woman to deal with.

As she rubbed the bulge in my jeans, I had to assume she had no problem with sex, just with relationships, which only had me more intrigued in discovering why.

She leaned in toward my mouth, and I was all for

kissing her, but I'd far rather do it horizontally and naked, instead of standing by the front door.

Leaning down, I braced her weight on one shoulder and straightened.

As her feet left the ground, she squeaked, "What are you doing?"

"Carrying you to bed." Normally I'd have asked first, but given she'd already unbuttoned my jeans and was in the process of sliding her hand inside my underwear before I'd hoisted her up, I didn't think she'd mind. "Problem?"

"No."

I couldn't see the pout, but I heard it in her tone.

She didn't like not being in charge. I could tell that about her already. But she didn't fight me now. Probably because I was taking her exactly where she knew we'd end up the moment I'd opened that door and she'd attacked me. Not that I was complaining. Of all the attacks I'd been involved in during my lifetime, this was by far the most—make that the *only*—pleasurable one.

Robert's guestrooms put the rooms at some five-star hotels to shame. When I'd arrived a few days ago, I'd settled into the bedroom I always stayed in when I visited him. The room I'd been using ever since my life had taken a surreal turn on that day we'd met those many years ago.

But in all the times I'd visited, I'd never once brought a woman to bed here.

As Robert's guest, I'd always come to spend time with him. But for the first time, he wasn't here while I was.

I ignored any shadow of guilt as I carried Joanne to the bed and dropped her onto the king-sized mattress. Robert wouldn't mind my guest being here. In fact, I was pretty sure he'd approve wholeheartedly.

"You going to close those curtains?" she asked, eyeing the wall of windows that faced the moonlit ocean.

"I like to wake up with the sun."

She cocked up one brow.

I back peddled on that decision and reached for the button next to the bed. "But I'll close them tonight." With a soft electric *whir* the curtains moved together.

"Thank you."

"You're welcome." The politeness of our conversation didn't match my actions as I opened the button and zipper on her fitted trousers and yanked them down her oh-so-long legs.

The lace panties followed the pants as I dropped both onto the floor next to the bed, before I dove between her legs headfirst.

Hell, I was a SEAL. Diving was part of the program. I didn't have long to be entertained with my own cleverness as I got my first taste of Joanne on my tongue.

She sucked in a sharp breath when my mouth made contact with her core, which only inspired me to work harder, drive her further.

I planned to push her all the way to a mind-numbing orgasm with my mouth and then slide inside for one of my own.

My plan worked. She came apart in seconds. No exaggeration.

I knew I was good, but I wasn't that good. This woman had to be primed and ready before I ever touched her to have a hair-trigger orgasm that rocked her, me and the bed we were on so quickly.

Her cries bounced off the walls of the cavernous room and I enjoyed every decibel. It was like a shot of testosterone, making me impossibly harder. But I was glad Robert was a state away and not inside the house.

When she finally untangled her fingers from my hair, I lifted my head and got a good look at her flushed face.

I might have sacrificed some hair for the encounter but seeing her look like that was well worth it. Sated yet hungry for more. Relaxed but on edge as she watched me.

If she was wondering what I was going to do next, she needn't have. There was only one way this night was going to go. I reached for the bedside table and pulled out a box of condoms.

Her brow cocked up. "Hmm. You're prepared."

I heard the attitude in her tone just as I saw her withdraw emotionally.

Was this jealousy? Did she think I had so many women in this bed that I kept a stash of condoms at the ready?

I could have told her Robert, the consummate host, supplied everything any of his guests could ever want. There were tampons and prescription sleeping pills provided too, along with toothbrushes and toothpaste. I could have told her, but I didn't.

She was getting pissed and, sick motherfucker that I was, I liked a little fire in a woman.

Sex with her soft and satisfied would only be surpassed by sex with her spitting mad.

"Be glad I am prepared," I told her.

I was naked and sheathed in seconds. Then it was time to prove to her why she should be glad I was armed with condoms.

Spreading her legs wide, I pushed inside her slick heat. I had every intention of fucking her until she couldn't think. As it turned out, I was the one affected.

The moment she surrounded me I felt it. A connection. A feeling of finally finding . . . home, for lack of a better word.

Shit. This wasn't turning out to be some mindless fuck. But that's exactly what it needed to be.

Yeah, I could enjoy her company for a few days until Robert returned. And even then, maybe she and I could get together at her place, or hell, on the beach. Or even here, if I wanted to deal with the old man sticking his nose in my personal life once he knew I'd had an overnight guest.

But after that, when my leave was over and I went back to real life, that would be it. She, this, would be a memory. One that I could let my mind return to but not repeat.

"What's wrong? You all right?" she asked.

I realized I'd frozen. Sunk deep inside her with my hands hooked beneath her knees and her gaze on me, I'd been thinking so hard I'd forgotten to move.

Of all the problems I had, thinking too much had never been one of them. Particularly during sex.

"Nah. I'm good. More than good." The last came out on a growl as I got my head—and my cock—back in the game.

If this thing between us was going to be a limited run, I was going to enjoy it to the fullest.

I leaned low and latched on to her neck, kissing then nipping her flesh as I thrust hard and fast.

I'd jerked off to images of this woman more times than I wanted to admit in the short amount of time I'd known her. That had to help me hold back now as I loved her for an impressively long time, if I did say so myself.

Finally, I hit the point of no return. With the sensation of fire and ice shooting through me, I held deep and came hard.

Only after I'd collapsed over her, still buried inside, did I feel it. Her muscles rhythmically gripping my spent cock.

Her breaths came short and fast, ramping up to soft cries.

I pressed closer, holding myself inside even as I threatened to slip out. I closed my eyes and concentrated on the feel of this woman coming around me. I enjoyed every pulse and held my breath as I waited longer and longer for the next one to come until finally there were no more.

"Fuck." I breathed out the cuss before lifting my head to get a look at her face. "That . . . you . . . I . . ."

"Spit it out, big boy." Her lips quirked up in a smile, the cocky woman in charge back in full force. Her attitude had me starting to get hard again.

I groaned. "We're doing this again."

"Can you?" Her icy stare dropped low where I'd just pulled out of her and was in the process of snapping off the used condom.

I heard the challenge in her voice and I was more than up for it. "Just watch me."

Covered and ready, I flipped her over onto her stomach. She squeaked along with the mattress as I lifted her hips high and knee walked behind her. "I hope you don't have any plans for the rest of the night."

"I have to be on set early in the morning."

"Don't worry. I should be done by then." I grinned, plunging inside and forcing a breath out of her.

"I do need to sleep at some point," she gasped, breathing hard as I set a fast pace.

"Do you though?" I questioned.

She laughed. That was all the answer I needed.

I eyed the box on the nightstand. It was only a three-pack. Apparently, Robert didn't have as much faith in my stamina as I did. But I was betting the other guestroom was similarly stocked. And if not? Then we'd just have to get creative.

In fact, I really liked that idea. So much potential.

"I'm very glad you stumbled onto the wrong property," I said as I reached my hand around and slid it down her belly.

She sucked in a breath between her teeth as I found her clit, before she said, "Me too."

4

JOANNE

I'll freely admit that I'm addicted to coffee. And I was fine with that. But the realization that after only three nights spent in Jacob's bed had caused me to be addicted to the man did not sit well with me. Not at all.

How did I know I was addicted? Because after being away from him for just a few days, I felt his absence. Felt it to my core. And not just between my legs either. I missed seeing him at the end of a long workday. Missed the release—the escape—he provided. Our time together gave me what I hadn't realized was missing in my workaholic life.

I should have never gone back that second night. Or the third. I definitely shouldn't have spent the whole night with him every damn time. And I really, really shouldn't have let him cook me breakfast that second morning.

That act felt even more intimate than all we'd done in

bed. And in the pool . . . and in the hot tub. We attempted it in the sauna and almost died from the heat.

But it all paled compared to the time we did it in the screening room while my favorite guilty pleasure played on the giant screen.

Why had I told him I loved *Outlander*?

Sitting on Jacob, naked, in that big leather recliner, and letting him make me come while I watched a larger-than-life Jamie make love to Claire was completely over the top—and hot as hell. I'd loved every second of it and felt my cheeks burn every time I thought of it.

This was bad. Very, very bad. But I'd obviously brought it all on myself.

I couldn't fall for Jacob. I barely knew him. Not that that mattered. I'd known my ex-fiancé plenty well after a decade and he'd dumped me out of the blue.

I'd never recover fully from that betrayal. The scars had hardened my heart, I'd thought to the point I'd never be tempted to let another man in.

But I was tempted by Jacob.

Shit.

I should go home and take out that engagement ring and look at it good and hard. It was the reminder I needed to reinforce what I knew but was in danger of forgetting. I couldn't trust men. I couldn't trust love.

Yet here I was, turning into Jacob's driveway rather than the beach house where we were filming what I hoped would be my company's next hit reality show.

After being away from set for days putting out fires in

the main office in Burbank, I should head directly to the beach house and check in with Maria.

I chastised myself—for so many reasons—for not doing exactly that as I rang the bell at the gate of the house next door. For the first time the gate was actually closed, which seemed strange since it had always been open before.

"Hello?" An older man's voice responded to my buzz, which threw me completely.

"Um, hi. I was looking for Jacob—" I stopped when I realized I'd never learned his last name.

Jesus. I knew his body. The taste. The smell. Every tattoo and scar, but not his last name. What exactly did that say about me?

And now that I thought about it, why did he have so many scars anyway?

Christ, was he like a squatter? A vagabond who cased empty beach houses and moved in while the owners were away? My trust issues were on high alert as I waited for the man in the house to ask, *Jacob, who?*

"I'm sorry. Jacob left. But I'm certain he'll be very disappointed he missed *you*." At the flirty tone in the man's raspy voice my gaze flew to the speaker and I realized there was a camera. He could see me but I couldn't see him. "Can I give him a message?"

"No. Thank you. No need. Sorry to have bothered you." I had the window up and the car in reverse as quickly as I could, fleeing from the scene of my humiliation.

Jacob was gone. No warning. No goodbye. Not even a note saying, *it's been fun.*

The last thing I was in the mood to do was be on set and have to deal with the cast and crew. But I knew it was what I needed to do. Throw myself into work and forget all about Jacob.

5

JACOB

"Hey," I said when Robert answered my call.

"Well, hello there. Are you back?" Robert asked.

"Just got to base."

"I must say it's quite rude they disturbed you on your vacation."

I laughed at Robert's ire on my behalf.

Unfortunately, my command didn't give a fuck I was on leave. When I got called up, I had to go, vacation or not. At least this had been a quick one. In and out. Just how I liked it.

"By my calculations," Robert continued, "they owe you another week off to make up for the time they stole from you. So come back and spend it here."

I chuckled again. "It doesn't work that way. I'll have to put in a request for any time outside of my original leave."

"Stupid rules." He sighed. "Still, you weren't due back until Monday, correct? You could come back for the weekend."

"I could." I smiled, knowing he'd talk me into driving there tonight even if the last thing I wanted to do was be in any sort of vehicle after the transport from hell I'd endured the past twenty-four hours.

"I'd think you want to come back given the vixen who came looking for you yesterday."

"What's that now?" I asked as he captured my full attention.

"Blonde. Late thirties, maybe. Asked for you by name. Didn't want to leave a message."

The smile spread wide across my face. Joanne had come looking for me. But crap. I'd left without even a goodbye. That wasn't going to sit well with her. "What did you tell her?"

"That you'd left."

"Nothing else?"

"No, nothing else. You're always reminding me I can't go around telling people you're a SEAL. Like it's some state secret."

"Shit." I drew in a breath. "Did she look mad I wasn't there?"

"She didn't look happy. So, are you going to tell me whom she is?"

I wanted to say no. The word was on the tip of my tongue, but Robert was a friend, not to mention he'd always been insanely generous to me. And I had taken advantage of his hospitality with Joanne. In all sorts of places.

"She works for the production company making that reality show next door. She got lost and showed up at your place by mistake. So I gave her directions to the right address."

"And is that all you gave her? Directions?"

I let out a huff, digging my heels in to preserve what was left of my privacy. But the reality was Robert was currently my closest—hell, my *only*—link to Joanne. I should have gotten her damn phone number. I'd figured we had time for all that. I should have known better. I was paying for that assumption now.

"You serious about that invitation for this weekend?" I asked.

"Ah ha! You two did do more than just talk."

"I'm not going to answer that."

"Then I'll just go count the condoms in the guest room," he threatened.

I bit out a vile curse, which only had Robert laughing. Defeated, I said, "Fine. Yes. We spent a few nights together. And I assumed we'd have a few more."

"Then you got recalled," he finished my thought.

"Yup."

"And? I'm assuming since she came looking for you that you hadn't told her you were leaving."

"I don't have her number."

"And your legs don't work? You couldn't walk next door and leave a note?"

I knew Robert's stance on my generation's reliance on cell phones. I wasn't in the mood to argue it now when I was clearly in the wrong. For not getting her number. For not leaving her a note or something. I had only one thing in my defense. "I didn't have any time to do anything except grab my bag—which luckily I keep packed—and jump in the car. We went wheels up as soon as I hit the airfield."

"Then I guess you need to get your ass back here and explain that to her."

"I think you're right. Are you sure it's okay if I come back tonight? I don't want to put you out—"

Robert let out a string of obscenities. "Jesus. You're not putting me out. You can move in here if you want to. You saved my life. If you hadn't been jogging by Hotel Coronado when I had that heart attack, I'd be dead."

"Someone else would have administered CPR if I hadn't been there. But thank you. I wouldn't mind spending the weekend with you." And I certainly wouldn't mind running into Joanne so I could explain.

"So get your ass in your car and get over here. I've got a bottle already open and I can't guarantee there will be any left by the time you arrive."

I rolled my eyes, not worried since I knew he bought all his favorite liquor by the case. "All right. I'll be there in a few."

"A few *hours* you mean. I don't know why you can't just jump in a helicopter. Don't you have a few of those around there?"

I shook my head at his assumptions. "See you soon."

"Jacob?"

"Yeah?"

"If I were you, I'd bring your dress uniform with you."

I frowned. "Why?"

"No woman can resist a man in a uniform. You want to woo her back, you wear that. Trust me."

I laughed out loud at the suggestion. "If you say so. I'm hanging up now."

Disconnecting I shoved clean shorts, underwear and a couple of T-shirts into my duffle for the next few days. My swimsuit was already at Robert's house where I'd forgotten it hanging in the shower stall drying when I'd rushed out.

I turned to leave when Robert's crazy theory had me turning back and walking to my closet.

What the hell. Why not? My uniform might not help, but it couldn't hurt.

6

JOANNE

"This is boring. A bunch of Millennials sitting around drinking is not gonna beat last season's ratings."

Maria stared at me, a frown marring her brow. "We've got Truth or Dare Giant Jenga scheduled for tomorrow morning—"

"Move it up to tonight."

She cringed. "They're pretty drunk."

"Exactly." I met her stare head on, not backing down.

Maybe I had been taking my bad mood out on everyone since finding Jacob gone, but I was still the executive producer. It was my reputation on the line if this show tanked because we'd somehow chosen the most lackluster cast on earth.

Maria finally reached for her radio. "Set up the Jenga. We're moving it up to tonight instead of tomorrow."

"Um, all right. I'm on it," her assistant's reply came through the radio.

Satisfied, I nodded. "Thank you."

"No problem. It's a good idea." She turned to look at me, then looked past me. "What the hell?"

I spun to see what was happening. Hopefully it was something ratings worthy. And if it was, there had better be a camera catching it.

What I saw had my mouth going dry. Jacob in full dress uniform was walking up the path from the driveway.

Maria and I weren't the only ones to spot him. The formerly dead cast finally woke up and took notice.

"Who's that?"

"Oh. My. God."

"Is he joining the cast?"

I ignored the girls' comments and just stared, speechless, as Jacob walked across the courtyard and toward me.

"Do we know this SEAL?" Maria asked, apparently noticing the trident he wore just as I had.

The question knocked me out of my stupor. "I do."

"Hmm. *Is* he a new cast member?" Maria asked, with more than a bit of interest.

"Definitely not." The last thing I wanted was Jacob on set around the females of this cast.

My jealousy was not a good sign. I could not let myself be swayed by this man in his showy uniform. I could not be with him again. More, I knew I couldn't bear being hurt again.

He approached me with his hat literally in his hand, his head hung low. "Hi."

I swallowed and somehow managed to say, "Hi."

He glanced around at the circus surrounding us. "Can we talk?"

I shook my head. "I don't think we—"

"If you don't want to talk then just listen. I didn't tell you what I am, what I do, and that's my fault. I should have. I would have."

He took a step closer and I saw the sincerity in his eyes, in addition to the rows of ribbons on his chest.

"I stupidly assumed we'd have more time. But then I got recalled and had literally hours to drive back to base. I know you're mad and you have every right to be. I'm so sorry." He moved even closer, reaching out to run his hand down my arm. "I'll do better in the future."

"The future?"

"Yeah. If you'll let me. Coronado isn't all that far from here. And it seems my friend is all for me being next door as often as possible—"

Jacob didn't get to finish his sentence as I leapt forward and crashed my lips against his.

Clearly, I was going to have to schedule an extra therapy session for this month because it seemed like a good idea to kiss him. To forgive him. To enter into a no-doubt ill-fated relationship with an active duty Navy SEAL stationed at a base over three hours away.

While I kissed him, every one of the many issues I had

with being with him, plus any I could come up with in the future, fled from my brain.

"This is just like that old movie!" one of the cast squealed.

"It's so romantic!"

The comments, and the accompanying discussion it spurred, reminded me we weren't alone. I pulled back, but not far.

"Does this mean you forgive me?" he asked.

I didn't answer. I had a question of my own. "You said you didn't do relationships."

"I was wrong. As it turns out, I do." His gaze held mine. "What about you?"

My heart fluttered with hope that scared the hell out of me. In spite of the fear, I said, "I might be willing to give it a try."

He leaned in and touched his forehead to mine. "That's good to hear. Maybe we should get out of here and discuss it."

Jacob looked like he was anticipating more than just talking. I know I was.

"Okay." Nodding, I turned to Maria.

She dismissed me with a wave of one hand. "Go. I got this."

"Thanks." I glanced back to him, struggling to get my footing in this new situation. "I just want you to know. If you hurt me, trident or no trident, I will destroy you."

To my surprise, he laughed. "There's the spitfire I know and love. And I wouldn't have it any other way."

The spitfire I know and love . . .
Love. I wanted that again. With him.
Risk be damned.

SEALS IN PARADISE BY CAT JOHNSON

HOT SEAL, DIRTY MARTINI Clay & Tasha
HOT SEAL, TIJUANA NIGHTS Zach & Gabby
HOT SEAL, RUNAWAY BRIDE Nick & Dani
HOT SEAL, HEARTBREAKER Brian & Alicia
HOT SEAL, COLD WATER Joanne & Jacob
HOT SEAL, UNDER PRESSURE Stefan & Shelly

ABOUT THE AUTHOR

Cat Johnson is a top 10 New York Times bestseller and the author of the USA Today bestselling Hot SEALs series. She writes contemporary romance featuring sexy alpha heroes and the sassy heroines brave enough to love them. She is known for her unique marketing. Cat has sponsored pro bull riders, owns a collection of camouflage and western wear for book signings, and has used bologna to promote romance novels.

Find Cat's complete backlist at CatJohnson.net

Get subscriber exclusive deals and content. Join Cat's inner circle at *CatJohnson.net/news* for email alerts.

Made in United States
Orlando, FL
30 September 2024